Plenteous Grace

Barbara Belseth

A Pandemic

Valborg Kristiane Lee heard the rattle of the coroner's truck before she saw it, for it was only an old Model T truck with a sloppily painted sign 'Coroner' on the side. Valle wondered how many bodies were already in there.

"Dear God help us," she breathed.

She watched two men with white masks covering their faces, jump out and pull an empty stretcher from the back and quickly enter the house across the street.

"Truck, Truck," little David yelled excitedly, waving a stick in his sister's face. Valle took their little hands and led them to the shade and watched and waited. She did not have to wait long. The men soon returned with a covered corpse on the stretcher and slid it into the truck, and too casually jumped back into their seats and drove off. Valle waited a bit longer and soon Pastor Gabrielsen, also wearing his white cloth mask, walked out.

"Oh, Pastor, who was it? Who was it who

died?" She called from a distance.

"It was him. Jim. He got sick two days ago and died early this morning. Catherine seems to have survived and is better. The children are recovering. My wife has been over there, they have food and Catherine's family is coming up from Providence soon to take care of them. Of course, there will be no funeral." He paused.

"Mrs. Lee, a woman in your condition should stay inside. Be careful."

"Yes, of course, I am so sorry, thank you. Of course, you are right. "This is all so sad, so tragic," she turned and said, "In the house, in the house." She ushered her whining children back into the house.

"Papa will be home soon, in the house." A feeling of helplessness washed over her as she looked down at little David and Harriet playing. The baby inside her gave a kick and she returned to her chores. When would this be over? When would the dying stop? In her short life living here and in Norway, she had never seen or heard of anything like this flu epidemic. Now with her own young children and another soon to come, her life and the lives of her children seemed so fragile and in danger. There was nothing to do, no way to avoid this random illness and no way to escape this silent, invisible killer.

Valle could see the fear in her mother's eyes, even as her mother comforted her and told her not to worry, that life was in God's hands. He would watch over them. Sure, Valle thought. And was God watching out for all the other pregnant women who died? Was he watching when that family died in Woonsocket? An entire family, mother, father, two children, found dead in their home by a neighbor, suffocated, drowning in their phlegm in their own beds. So quick. Ruthlessly cutting down the young and healthy in a matter of hours.

Her family tried to mitigate the risk, her husband and mother especially. They tried to encourage her to have faith and not worry. Her father, Oluf, less stoical by nature than the rest of the family, would regularly check on her. He simply offered solace. "How's my little girl today?" he would softly ask, tenderly patting her hand. "Don't worry. You haven't been near anyone who is sick. You are healthy. You'll both be fine."

But she was no fool. The very fact that she and Trygve were young and healthy, and she pregnant, put them at the greatest risk. Tears came to her and weariness overtook her as she sank into a chair. David snuggled at her side. What would she do if she lost any of them? What would they do without her? Would she live to see this new baby? Or what about her husband? What if she lost him? When would this terror end?

~

The children ran to their father when Trygve came home. "How are my little ones? And how are you, Valle? How are you feeling?" He leaned over and gave her a light kiss.

"Jim died. The coroner came with his truck and took him away this morning. We watched." Valle turned her face away from her husband and sat down.

"Oh, no," he whispered. "This is really spreading. Oh that is tough. Poor Catherine." Trygve shook his head and looked over at his wife. "You know I think I have been hopeful and maybe denying it, that this flu would come so close to home."

"The whole family is sick. I spoke briefly to Pastor Gabrielsen. Catherine's sister is coming to take care of them."

"Not that you would even think of going near anyone in need, my dear."

"Oh, I know, I know."

After dinner they read the papers. The Boston papers reported that emergency units of nurses and physicians reported to Boston from Rhode Island, Maine, and Toronto. Volunteers had sewn over three thousand face masks to ship to Camp Devons where hundreds of soldiers were sick. In Worcester Mayor Holmes was attempting to advance improved public hygiene practices, including suppressing public spitting on sidewalks. Church services there were canceled for the coming weeks. Even the Swedish Covenant Church was canceling services this weekend. Emergency hospitals were springing up and full as soon as they were open. The grim reports in the news included totals of the dead from each town, lists of church services and activities canceled, and the latest casualties and of course, news from the front in Europe.

October progressed and the reports from both Europe and Boston improved as the number dying from flu began to subside; talk of armistice came from Europe. The Lee family remained healthy as

Valle waited. Valle became a little numb to the continuous influenza news. Between borrowing from Kristen, her sister-in-law, and others, she had a large pile of diapers and baby blankets to organize again and again. Her mother, with her graying hair tied back and her blue eyes, eager to help, bought her groceries for her and made sure she ate an apple every day. Her baby was growing and safe so far.

Finally on a cool morning in late October, little Harriet ran up the hill holding up her white nightgown, her tousled golden brown hair flying in her face, and into her grandparents' house. "Besta, Far, come, come! Mama's going to have the baby! Mama's going to have the baby!" She jumped up and down, waving her arms and clapping her hands, "The baby!" Her grandmother flew out of the door toward the cottage that backed up to their duplex.

"Harriet, get Tante Kristen."

Harriet gleefully ran through the back porch to the kitchen of the duplex. Kristen, her own rosy faced babe on her hip, came into her kitchen with a smile.

"Well, her time has come. I could hear you upstairs." She smiled. "Harriet, where's your father?"

"Momma told him, 'Go to get the doctor'. He left and Momma is in bed, and David is there, and Momma told me to get Besta and tell her the baby was coming and Besta ran to the house and I am here." She clapped her hands. "Can I hold your baby?"

"Maybe later. Right now, let's go get your brother. Would you like to spend the day with me? I bet you could help me make bread. Do you know how to knead dough?"

"Oh, yes. I can make bread. I help my Mama."

"Well, good. And it is best your father is not around. We don't need two patients." Kristen twisted her long blonde hair, pinned it up, threw a sweater on and took Harriet's hand.

"Will the doctor bring the baby?"

Kristen sighed, "Yes, the doctor will bring the baby. God willing, he'll be here with a healthy baby. You will have a new baby sister or brother."

She took Harriet's hand and, still carrying the baby, they walked down to the cottage to find Besta busy by the stove and Valle sitting up in bed. The women talked in hushed tones. Kristen took all the children back to her home and began the bread making for the day.

With the children gone, Valle shuffled back and forth in the kitchen talking to her mother, stopping when the contractions gripped her body. By the time Trygve returned with Dr. King, she was back in bed. Her mother rubbed her back as she moaned in pain. Trygve leaned over and held her hand, "How are you feeling?"

"Get out and go wait, dear, go."

Dr. King agreed, turning to Trygve, "Chris, you can leave now. Don't worry. We'll let you know as soon as the baby is here."

"Doc, I won't be far. What can I do? Is there anything I can do? Can I get you anything?"

"Chris, just take care of yourself for now. Don't worry, you'll be needed later. You won't be of any help here." He grabbed his friend's thick arm and led him out of the room.

Dr. King, a country doctor in the Blackstone River Valley in Massachusetts had treated Trygve for a broken leg that was slow to heal. During the many home visits, the doctor and patient had enjoyed their spirited political conversations so much that Chris began joining the doctor on his rounds and reading the news aloud to him. The doctor had been pleased to find in his invalid patient a likeminded man who was more than willing to read the newspapers and discuss the war news as he drove to his home visits. Trygve happily accompanied the doctor, reading aloud the latest news from the front as Dr. King drove the winding roads to treat the latest Quinsy throat or consumption. As a bonus, Dr. King could count on the mechanical skill of his patient whenever the car broke down, which was often. But happiest of all was Valle, who encouraged the arrangement to give her husband an outlet and opportunity to ride around the countryside with the doctor and get her husband out of the house and feeling useful.

Trygve now looked back at his wife going through childbirth for the third time and with tears in his eyes, "I love you, Valle." She waved her hand at him, clenching her teeth as the next contraction came.

"Go."

"I won't be far. If you need me, I'll come right away."

Christian Trygve Lee was solidly built with wide shoulders and a muscular body. Although not particularly tall, Trygve was a powerful presence in any room with blue eyes that looked you full in the face with confidence. Trygve had briefly taken up boxing back in Norway, but since he fainted at the mere hint of blood, his fighting career had come to a definitive end. And no one wanted him around for a birth.

Trygve left Norway as a young man with his skills as a machinist, coming to America to work in New England's factories and room with his aunt, Josephine Andersen. Years earlier, Josephine, now called Besta for grandmother, emigrated with her sailor husband Oluf and three children from Christiana (later renamed Oslo). There was work in the factories and the family settled with other European immigrants in the Blackstone River Valley. Josephine had kept boarders and somehow managed to scrape together enough money to buy two small homes; a small duplex on West Street with a cottage in the backyard that faced onto Ironstone Street. Thrown into the deal, across from the duplex, was a small lot next to the railroad tracks where the family's garden flourished. Beside taking in boarders, Josephine provided for the family by raising chickens, and commandeering as much of her husband's pay as she could before Oluf spent it all drinking every payday.

Trygve had arrived in the port of Boston with two other young men from Norway traveling together to Millville. The three managed to make their way by train to Millville and then to his aunt's boarding house. Overwhelmed with the new experience of being in a foreign country, and surrounded by people speaking English, the young men were comforted by their new landlady who had a hearty stew ready for them. There at his aunt's boarding house the homesick teenager met his cousin Valle and the two had fallen in love.

Trygve's family back in Norway, particularly his own father, were not happy with the wedding plans. Trygve was furious when he received letters from his mother and family members back in Norway warning him of the dangers of marrying a cousin, even though they were first cousins through only one grandparent. What would their children be like? Their children could be imbeciles or suffer from deformities. Weren't there any other Norwegians to marry there in America? How far was it to Minnesota? Perhaps he should move and find a bride in New York or Chicago. Weren't there more Norwegians in those places?

Now a young man in a new country and making his own life, Trygve had steamed with anger that his family back in Norway did not trust his judgment. No one in America, of course, dared disagree with him to his face. So distraught was he by his family's criticism, that when he went before a judge to become a citizen, he changed his name. The once Trygve Christian Svendsen, dropped his surname and became Christian Trygve Lee, Lee being a Norwegian farm name associated with the family. The wedding went on. Mr. and Mrs. Christian Trygve Lee were married in the house on West Street Christmas day 1912.

Trygve soon found a new job and the young couple moved to Cambridge for a short time. Valle, who had grown up living in the center of Christiana, loved living in the city and being able to go into Boston on the trolley. There one summer morning, Valle, pregnant with her first child, sat on a park bench on the Boston Commons watching a very American nanny playing with her two charges as they ran up and down the wide walkways of the park, their colorful hair bows bouncing away as they ran. Obviously sisters, the girls had thick chestnut hair flowing over their shoulders and were dressed fashionably for play. The older sister wore a blue seersucker drop waist with white collar and cuffs and the little one wore a coral-colored pleated dress with bloomers. The nanny was a sprite of a young girl with freckles. Her bright red hair tucked up under a navy bonnet with her navy dress neat and trimmed with navy grosgrain. The nanny had called to the little girls with a lovely lilt to her voice that Valle could not quite place. "Harriet, Dorothy, not so fast. I can barely keep up with ye." Valle had enjoyed watching the three of them, so carefree with each other, and imagining her own children happily playing one day. Their names sounded so musical, so American, from the lips of this bright and easy-going nanny. Valle's children would be American and she would give her children American names.

Later, the young family moved back home to Millville and the family compound and Trygve found work in the rubber mill. And so on this October day in 1918, there was great relief, for many reasons, when a healthy baby girl joined her brother David and sister Harriet. Dorothy Esther Lee squirmed and cried in her mother's arms as her parents, grandparents, aunt and siblings all admired her, happily checking all her parts and counting her toes.

Dr. King wearily shook Trygve's hand in congratulations. "Just stay away from any crowds for a while more. I don't have to tell you, I know. This flu could end soon. Let's hope. The numbers of deaths seem to be decreasing. In the meantime, Valle will do fine. You know where to find me if you need anything."

"Well doc, I hope I don't have to call you again for any of the family. Not any time soon." And Trygve would not be calling his friend. But the doctor would be coming again.

"The flu epidemic began to subside in mid-October. Later estimates put the number of Massachusetts flu deaths at 45,000 from Sept. 1, 1918 to Jan. 16, 1919, but those are now considered low."

http://www.newenglandhistoricalsociety.com/the-1918-flu-epidemic-kills-thousands-in-new-england/

Saint Vincent

The train rattled through the rolling hills toward Worcester. Valle sat staring out the window, with an occasional tear running down her cheek. She and Oluf, her father, were taking the train to Worcester and Saint Vincent Hospital to visit her husband. Her father put his head back and snoozed. For the first time since her husband took ill, she had time for her own thoughts and fears. And the fear ate at her in the pit of her stomach, slowing churning and destroying her future, her peace. But what could she have done differently? Nothing.

Trygve complained off and on of pain that week but had not slowed down. Then at church just that Sunday, Valle was drinking in the sermon on God's love when she noticed her husband next to her in the pew squirming, taking out his handkerchief, wiping his face, and giving her a painful look. As they stood for the last hymn, he told her they had to go right home. He was feeling sick. When they got home, he curled up on the bed in pain.

She thought he was getting better, but in the morning, the pain was worse. Trygve shivered under the blanket, burning with fever. Dr. King had come. The doctor had examined Trygve, asked a few questions and, the color draining from the doctor's face, he stood tall over the bed, in the tiny room. For a moment the doctor just looked at them, Valle and her and parents, gathered there, silently searching his face for hope.

"I am afraid that Trygve has suffered a ruptured appendix. He is very ill. I want you to get him to my office by noon today." Then he turned to his moaning friend lying there, his voice shaking, "I'm going to take good care of you." And the doctor was gone.

In a daze, Valle bathed her husband, gave him a fresh shirt, and prayed. Oluf planned and found a ride for them. Valle, Oluf and a very sick Trygve had made it to the doctor's office as told, while Besta stayed and watched the children.

Dr. King arrived at his full infirmary and took Trygve back to be examined yet again. Valle and Oluf waited in the crowded waiting area as a shiny black truck emblazoned with white letters "County Coroner" pulled up. Dr. King called them back to the examining room where her husband lay covered in white linens. Trygve looked up at his wife and barely mumbled, "Dr. King knows what to do, Valle. I trust him."

"Chris needs help that I cannot give him here. We need to get him to Saint Vincent Hospital in Worcester right away. He needs surgery. I've made arrangements to get him on the next train to Worcester. The ambulance is here now to take him to the train station and there is no time to wait."

"No, no. I will not let you take him away." Valle was startled by her own voice, "We can take care of him at home. No, I can't lose him. You can't take him from me. No." She had sobbed, throwing herself on her husband. Dr. King had gently pulled her away and into the hall.

Holding her shoulders, he looked into her eyes and spoke softly, "Mrs. Lee, if you take Chris home now, you take him home in a box. Our only hope is to get him to the hospital for surgery as soon as we can." The gurney was already being rolled into the room. Trygve was quickly transferred, rolled out and into the waiting 'ambulance', on his way to the train station and Saint Vincent Hospital. And her husband was gone.

Would she see him again? There was never a goodbye. Would they arrive now at the hospital to find him dead, or alive? Hospitals and surgery often meant death. Although no one wanted to say it aloud, the family all knew that most people died from a ruptured appendicitis. Valle had gone home and alone in their bedroom, thrown herself on the floor in desperate prayer. Her beloved husband was in God's hands, and the hands of the surgeons. The sense of dread and despair was now slowly being replaced by a seed of hope as she traveled closer to her destination.

She pictured the scene at their arrival at the hospital. *She would be cheerfully greeted by the nurses, thrilled at her arrival. "We've been waiting for you Mrs. Lee."*

"Oh, I am ready to take him home. His children miss him. He needs some good food to

recover." The English words for her argument to take him home slipped easily off her lips. The nurses all agreed, "Your husband is eager to see you and go home. He will do so much better with your care and back home with his family." Trygve would be sitting up, recovering with a smile. So glad to see her. She would quickly take over ....

"Union Station, Worcester " the train came to a clanking halt. Sunlight filtered through the soaring stained glass ceiling of the station as they passed through the crowd of travelers. The father and daughter found the right trolley and glumly made their way to Saint Vincent Hospital, high on a hill in the city.

The red brick hospital towered six stories with gleaming white porches and balconies outlined in more white trimming on the lower stories. Sweeping lawns encompassed the grounds. A tall covered portico with white columns then led into the cavernous reception area. With her father meekly following her, Valle walked up to the reception desk and stood silently, waiting for the nun, who was diligently recording information in a notebook, to look up. Finally, the nun, from under her white habit and cap, looked up and smiled.

"Can I help you?"

"Yes, I am here to see my husband. Christian Lee, he arrived yesterday. Dr. King from Blackstone is our doctor."

"Please take a seat. I'll be with you as soon as I can."

Valle and her father found seats and waited.

Valle looked around and wondered what other people were there for. She watched the clock and waited. Finally she rehearsed the words in her mind, and went again to the desk to beg for some information, but just then a young nurse appeared,

"Mrs. Lee? I'm going to take you to his room. Christian Lee? Correct, he is your husband?"

"Yes, yes, we've come from Millville this morning." Valle was greatly relieved to hear that her husband was indeed alive. The nurse led them down the hall, upstairs and through more halls until they came to a small waiting area at the corner of the hospital where they were to wait. Oluf looked out the windows at the view of the seemingly silent city sprawling below, life going on, trolleys, buses, trains, and people moving through their day. Here the only sounds were indistinct voices and muffled movements. Valle sat on the edge of a seat, waiting again.

Another nurse approached with a smile.

"Mrs. Lee, Mr. Lee will be glad to see you. Come this way. You must realize that he just had surgery yesterday," she spoke cheerily as she led them down the hallway. "He may not be too talkative. He's still very sleepy. He will be moved to the regular ward soon and the doctor should be in to see you shortly."

Eagerly, Valle and Oluf followed her to his room. Christian Trygve Lee lay motionless and pale in the white bed, covered with white crisp looking sheets and covers.

"Oh, Valle," his voice was weak, "You came. You came. I'm still alive." He barely cracked a small smile. "God's not through with me yet." They spoke in hushed tones. The doctor came.

"Mrs. Lee, Your husband is recovering very well from his surgery. He will need to stay with us to completely recover from the serious infection and operation."

The doctor went on to explain the surgery, the drain from the wound, and the weeks of recovery time needed. But Valle was content to watch her husband's chest move up and down and notice the ever so slight pink in his otherwise ashen face as he slipped in and out of sleep.

~

Early spring in New England is much like winter, but with the hope of newness and warmth soon to come. Trygve continued to recover in the care of the nuns and nurses. Valle was usually able to get a ride on the weekends. Dr. King checked in on him. Rev. Holgren visited regularly, often giving Valle a ride too.

Trygve was moved to a bed on the floor with other patients. Bundled up in his chair, his visitors could wheel him out to get some fresh air, or enjoy the sunshine in the enclosed porch where he viewed the city below in its old, gray winter garb, not yet bursting into spring.

Finally, after 6 weeks of recovery, the day came and Valle and her father climbed into the pastor's car as they made the last trip to Saint Vincent Hospital to bring Trygve home.

Valle walked through the gracious entrance.

"Mrs. Lee, is Chris going home today?"

"Yes Sister Anne, he is. Thank you so much

for everything."

The two women warmly shook hands and Valle and Oluf continued on to pick up their patient. They gathered his things, letters from Norway, all the cards, his Bible and clothes, and the nurses got a wheelchair.

"I'm OK, I'm going home, I can walk on my own," he protested.

"Mr. Lee, you are still a little weak," the nurse answered. She then looked at Valle with a smile, "He needs some good home cooking and his family now. He's been a tough patient. I bet he will be up to no good when he gets home!"

The nurses chuckled but a tear, a tear of joy, slipped down Valle's face as she thought back to her arrival so many weeks ago when she did not know if her husband was even alive. The doctor came by and wished them all well as he went on his rounds. Oluf pushed the wheelchair and off they went. Pastor Ogren waited in his Model T as the family piled happily into the car.

The Decision

Pastors and ministers hope and pray that their sermons impact their audience, but on Mother's Day in 1921, Pastor Ogren of the Scandinavian Congregational Church in Millville would have been surprised to learn how his sermon that Sunday would change the lives of an entire family.

Trygve Lee sat with his youngest child, asleep against his side. As the familiar organ music soared through the church and voices harmonized, tears came to his eyes as he thought about his sister Solviege. Death had come in the grip of that winter and too early in her young life. His father Hermann had written that despite their faith and hope in the resurrection, Trygve's mother, now having buried three of her seven children and lost him to America, was not recovering from her grief and suffered severely with melancholia.

Trygve smarted at his father's criticism when he married Valle. Trygve first met Valle there at the boarding house and the two soon fell in love with each other. Trygve never doubted his choice of a bride or forgot those who opposed him. But now his mother was sick with grief and Trygve, fresh from his own brush with death in this life, struggled to know how to respond.

As this father looked down at the curly head of his sleeping daughter, he was overcome to think of his mother's grief. No woman should carry this enormous burden of sorrow. Inge Svendsen had buried her two year old son when Trygve himself was a toddler. Then, not long after Trygve left for America, his brother Ingolf, just ten years old, succumbed to the flu. His sister Solveig had been such a comfort to his parents during those times. Then Solveig, just 17, came down with the flu last January and died a few weeks later. Now his father Hermann had written, and despite their past conflicts, was asking his son to help. His mother had suffered more than any mother should have to bear.

Hermann was not the type to easily ask for help. Trygve remembered leaving Christiana for America. There were sad goodbyes at home and then he and his father boarded the train headed toward his port of departure. There at the port in Christiana, across the street from the boarding dock, father and son had sat down to a last meal together. Tryge, heady with the new freedom awaiting him, ordered a beer.

"Son, in the name of God, I beg you not to begin your new life with drink. Please promise, at least let me have this little solace, promise you will not drink beer or alcoholic drinks. Let me have the comfort of knowing you will remain sober and live a Godly life, even if you are far away."

Trygve looked across the table at his father's face, for once softened with sadness and tears. His father leaned closer, "Son, you cannot run away from the Lord. May God go with you and may He keep you safe in the center of His will. in the palm of His hand. Please promise me you will not indulge in strong drink."

"All right, Pa, all right." Trygve pushed the glass away. The father and son had an emotional and unusually tender goodbye before Trygve boarded the ship. Trygve promised his father he would seek out a church and fellowship even in this new world of America. Now here he sat, so many years later so thankful for his father's admonishment and advice.

Today on Mother's Day, the pastor's voice rose and fell with emotion. Our Lord's mother, Timothy's mother, Moses' mother; every mother in the Good Book was an example of godly devotion. But this Swedish pastor gave his patriotic immigrant flock a sermon today focused on a mother who changed their world, a mother whose devotion, prayers, and selfless love changed one man and in so doing, changed America: Abraham Lincoln's mother.

With soaring detail and sweeping statements, the pastor told the story of Abraham Lincoln's selfless love for his stepmother. The pastor wiped tears from his own face as he quoted a grateful Lincoln singing the praises of motherly love. Trygve hung on every emotional appeal, every word, every nuanced phrase evoking gratitude for mothers, extolling the value of mothers. Nothing

21

could have spoken to his heart more than the story of a great American president, an American president, clinging to and remembering his mother's prayers. Tears streamed down his face. God was speaking to him. He must return to Norway and comfort his mother.

Valle knew she would struggle with worry all the time he was gone, but Valle, her parents, other relatives, all agreed that Inge's grief was exceptional and Trygve, the oldest son, should visit his family. Trygve booked his journey across the seas back to Norway and signed up to work on the ship during the crossing.

Valle knew she would struggle with worry all the time her husband was gone. At fourteen when her family had set out for America, she saw her voyage as an adventure until the ship began to move. Sea sickness swept over her for the voyage. Young, and overcome with excitement or sickness, she was free from fear of danger or tragedy. So she never really thought about any of the dangers of ocean travel at that time. Then only a month after arriving in America, the dramatic news of the sinking of the SS Norge not long after departing Norway was in all the newspapers. Valle read with dismay of the hundred and thirty-five souls drowning among the waves, rocks and skerries of the North Atlantic, mostly immigrants on their way to a new life, sucked into the deep or flailing in ferocious waves; the sea alive with drowning people and lifeboats full of children smashed to pieces against the doomed ship. And then years later came the horrific news of the Titanic.

But thousands of passengers made the Atlantic crossing safely every day. Of course ocean travel was safe, Valle consoled herself. Valle, her parents, other relatives, all agreed that Inge's grief was exceptional and Trygve, the oldest son, should visit his family. Valle kept her concerns and fears to herself. Trygve booked his journey across the seas back to Norway.

The family in America may have expected what would happen when Trygve returned from his visit to his family in Norway. Moved by the reunion with his parents and younger brother and sister, Trygve wanted to move back to Norway. Now Valle had lived in America longer than her husband and took some persuading. Economic recovery after The Great War was slow. The economy in the US was struggling with unemployment at a new high and Norway suffered from workers' strikes. But Valle's own brother, Tony, had offered Trygve an opportunity to work with him as he established his new business back in Norway selling coal in Christiana. Tony had assured Trygve that there was a future in his coal business. Norway had recently recovered rights to its own coal production and in 1921 there was a real future for coal sales in Christiana. Tony had lived in America himself and now returned to Norway so he seemed a trusted source of advice. Then when Valle's parents agreed to return to Norway for a visit and accompany them on the trip, Valle, with some misgivings, agreed. So the seven of them, Trygve and Valle, the three children, and her parents, Oluf and Josephine, would all voyage together and return to Norway and the Lees would attempt to reestablish their lives back in Norway.

Trygve booked passage on the SS Bergensfjord, a modern Norwegian Ocean liner that sailed nonstop between New York and Christiana. Trygve reassured his wife that the journey would be much shorter and more comfortable than her original journey to America which included transiting through England by train for Liverpool before crossing the Atlantic for Boston. And the Bergensfjord was a Norwegian vessel with a Norwegian crew and captain. The family would have small but private accommodations and of course she could count on help with the children from her parents during the voyage and the ship would not be crowded for the trip back to Norway. Trygve extolled the marvel of modern steamships and discussed the advantages and safety of the newest nautical technologies endlessly with anyone who would listen.

Valle sold off furniture, packed, and said her goodbyes. Her most prized furniture, a small parlor set of an overstuffed chair and sofa in two toned velour, was sold to a newly arrived Swedish family. The sturdy oak rocker she rocked her children in for so many hours was sold quickly. The ladies at church had a little coffee reception to say goodbye and Kirsten baked her delicious sweet rolls for the occasion. Valle had to say goodbye to her dear friend Margit who had dragged her to English classes at the Presbyterian Church just up the street. Her mother helped her organize and pack. The trunks were finally packed and ready to go. The family boarded the train in Millville the day before the departure and began their journey. Pastor Ogren was there at the train station with the Andersons, to say goodbye and give a blessing. Valle waved out the window and wondered if she would ever see Millville again.

On July 30, 1921 Captain Ole Bull piloted the SS Bergensfjord as it slid past the Statue of Liberty with 238 souls on board, including the Anderson and Lee family with their three precious children, and headed into the cold waters of the North Atlantic on the voyage to Christiania, Norway.

The Crossing

Despite her misgivings, Valle was beginning to look forward to being back in Christiania and remembers her childhood in the city she loved; the parks and fountains in summer and ice skating in the winter. Valle also remembers the smell of fresh ground coffee in her aunt's bake shop and the excitement of riding the trolleys with her brothers. Her family had been poor, but living right on Karl Johans Gate, the heart of Christiana, the city had been her playground. She could see herself walking once again on sidewalks bustling with fine ladies and prominent men in black coats and hats, smoking cigars as they argued and strolled down the boulevard toward the Stortinget. So now as the family boarded the ship and found their way to their cabin, she felt relief at actually getting the children on board and being underway. Standing on the deck, watching the New York City skyline disappear, as the ship reached open water and as the floor rolled beneath her feet, Valle began throwing up.

Trygve and Oluf had both spent more time at sea and did not suffer from sickness as much as the rest of the family. Valle and her mother tried lying still in their bunks, getting fresh air on deck, and taking the Mothersill's Seasickness Remedy pills from the ship's nurse, but nothing seemed to work for any length of time. As soon as everyone was well for a minute, the sound and smells of someone getting sick would send them all to a bucket. Valle found some comfort in the fresh air, sitting still on deck and sipping the hot beef broth offered in the dining hall, but with three young children to watch, the opportunity for that was rare. After a couple days at sea, the family finally seemed to settle in for a decent night's sleep. The ship's fog horn gave a low, plaintive warning, the adults in their bunks all breathed a sigh of relief and a prayer of thanksgiving for the quiet in their cabin as the children slept.

As the family slept peacefully, Captain Ole Bull stood on the bridge intently studying an officer's report. The SS Bergensfyord crawled at half speed through the fog and cold waters of the North Atlantic just 300 miles due south of Cape Race where North Atlantic icebergs neared the end of their voyage before finally breaking apart and melting. The souls on board were only about 100 miles from the icy grave of the Titanic not 10 years earlier. But this was August, summer, and shipping lanes should be safe from this stealthy danger. As most passengers slept, the men on deck, the wireless operator, even the coal stokers far below, any crewmember awake that night, were all aware of an unanticipated slow down.

Captain Bull hailed from the beautiful port city

of Bergen. A relatively young man to shoulder the responsibility of such a fine vessel, he came from a prominent family that, at least at first, was not enthusiastic about his choice of profession. But his calm determination and love of the sea had prevailed. Tonight, he needed those attributes as he analyzed the charts and data. The fog was no surprise this night but the water temperature was variable and alarmingly cold. The captain was concerned there could be ice in the vicinity. Tons of cargo heading for Norway would be late. The captain would be patient and wait for the fog to lift before resuming full speed. The foghorn hailed its low warning. There was no response. The SS Bergensfjord was alone tonight in this fog.

Trygve felt a jolt and woke with a start. Valle stirred and sat up. "What's happened?" As Trygve was about to reassure her, the fog horn sounded again. Then the ship was eerily still and silent. Trygve was up and pulling on pants when they heard people running.

On the bridge the captain and crew felt a bump. The ship lurched slightly and Captain Bull gave a curt order to shut all power. Passengers and crew ran to the deck and through the fog with torch lights could see an ice tower not 40 feet away from the ship. Crew members reported that an iceberg was visible off the starboard. Captain Bull calmly issued more orders. Officers made inspections, engineers were busy in the engine rooms keeping the steam engines from exploding now that the ship was not moving, the wireless operator was nervously sending distress calls, and stewards began knocking on passengers' doors.

Trygve and Valle were already dressed and getting the children up when they opened the door to the steward who was pounding on their door. "No damage to the ship but we appeared to have collided with an iceberg. The ship is stopped. Just to be on the safe side, the captain is order...um asking all passengers to put on life vests and meet on the lower deck promenade."

"We are all going to put on our life vests and go for a walk," Valle's voice wavered. She slid the yellow vests over the small frames of her children. But her hands were shaking so violently she could not fasten any of them. Trygve reached over and firmly held his wife's hands in his. "Harriet, David, we are going to put on these life jackets and go out on the deck and take a walk. Like the nice man said. Oh and here are Far and Besta to go with us," as the grandparents arrived, wide eyed and in their life vests. Trygve fastened and tied Valle's vest on her and then the sleepy children's life jackets.

The family joined the other passengers. With blankets and jackets wrapped over the life vests, the passengers all looked quite bundled up. There seemed to be more crew members than passengers on this westward voyage and all the steerage passengers filled a small area of the deck. The fog was thick and the summer sun had yet to rise. The ship and air were still.

An officer came to the huddle of passengers, "Ladies and gentlemen, I need to inform you that the ship has struck an iceberg. Our fine ship is not taking on water that we know of. Thank you for your cooperation. There is currently no order to evacuate the ship. Please remain here and keep your life jackets on. This is necessary at this time while we evaluate our situation. Please remain calm. Getting everyone up and ready to evacuate was a precaution. Thank you."

The children on the ship fell asleep in their parents' laps or snuggled in chairs next to them, their heads on laps. The bulky life vests and blankets enveloped and cushioned the small ones. The early morning became light. Crew members ran by, focused on their mission.

Then Captain Bull came striding into the Promenade deck and faced his passengers. Passengers stood up and gathered around.

"Good morning. I am Captain Bull. I am in command of this ship." He surveyed his audience.

"So I expect you all want to know why I had you all dragged out of your beds tonight. A few hours ago, in this fog, the ship collided with an iceberg. The ship was traveling at half speed and does not appear to have too great damage. We are not taking water. And this is a good thing." There was a general chuckle of relief.

"We can make a better assessment in daylight and when the fog lifts. But right now the ship is on or attached to the ice. We are stuck. In my assessment, trying to move the ship could cause more damage. And we do not want that." Captain Bull looked out over his attentive passengers, the souls in his care, and paused. "But as good Norwegians we all know something about ice in August. Ice melts! We will wait for the ship to naturally separate from the berg." There was another collective nervous chuckle and sigh of relief.

"I thank you for your cooperation. You are free to go to your cabins or other parts of the ship. However, I ask you to keep your life jackets on for now. Just in case. Thank you, God speed. I have a busy morning ahead of me." And he left.

The family quickly left the damp, cold deck and tried to put the children back to sleep. Trygve and Oluf headed up to the deck to catch the first glimpse of the iceberg and keep up with any news. Valle actually felt less sick and she and Besta took the children to breakfast after their eventful night and then headed out to the promenade deck with all the other passengers. The ship was still and the silence unnerving. There was only the sound of the ocean lapping the sides of the ship and the low, nervous conversation of passengers and crew. The fog lifted and the sun was suddenly bright. Off to the south two other steamships could be seen ominously circling back and forth and keeping close, but not too close, in case there was need for rescue. The iceberg shined in the sun, towering like a tall, slender shaft of glass. Valle sat Harriet on her lap and held her close.

"Look there. Look up. See that ice? Take a good look at this and remember. This is an iceberg. You may never see another one." Harriet looked up at the spire of ice and wondered why her mother found this so important. "And, you will always have this," Valle buried her face in her daughter's hair and wiped her tears, "You'll always have this memory, even when you are old, of this iceberg and this trip."

In the meantime, the wireless operator had sent out messages to both Christiana and New York City. That very day, newspapers on both continents would have news of a Norwegian passenger ship stranded on an iceberg and afloat in the North Atlantic, not far from the watery grave of the Titanic. The Providence, Rhode Island paper would pick up the story that seven members of one family from Millville, Massachusetts were floating helplessly on a ship that collided with an iceberg in the North Atlantic. The families on both sides of the Atlantic would pray and hope, and wonder why the Andersons and Lees had left in the first place.

The SS Bergensfjord spent that day floating rather helplessly attached to the hunk of melting ice. By that night the ship gave a lurch again as it freed itself from the berg. One of the screws, or propellers, had been damaged by the collision. Captain Ole Bull guided the ship slowly back to Christiana for repair. Captain Bull was presented with commendations for his wise handling of the ship during this dangerous collision and many thanks from the passengers. And Trygve and Valle had yet one more reason to thank God for each other and the very breath in their lungs.

Norway

Oluf and Josephine Andersen had raised their family in the city of Christiana. Their last address in Norway was right on Karl Johans Gate, the wide boulevard that ran through the center of the capital city. Olaf had gone months at a time off to sea as a merchant sailor. Josephine had survived raising three sons and a daughter in a 'basement' apartment working for a building owner and cleaning apartments. Olaf had traveled to exotic and tropical places, bringing back stories and a few pets. Josephine had not, as the story is told, been enamored with the monkey or parrot.

After Olaf visited America, though, he brought home a request for Josephine. Would his darling Phina move with him to America? He had met some Norwegians and been to a city he liked called Boston. There was work near there. Josephine agreed to move to America if he promised to give up sailing and stay home. So the Anderson family emigrated to America. Oluf and son Tony had gone ahead to find work and a place to live. In May of 1903, Josephine, Valle, Hans, and Rolf had traveled to England, crossed by train over to Liverpool, and boarded the Cunard Lines' SS Ivernia for Boston. Father and son Tony had been there on the dock in Boston to meet them on that bright spring day.

The family had found life in the small town of Millville pleasant enough. There was work in the rubber shop making boots, plenty of other immigrants moving to town including other Scandinavians. Many Norwegians found a home at the Scandinavian Congregational Church right in town. Other churches gave English classes and they had all made friends. Josephine soon figured out how to make money taking in boarders.

Now Valle may have sold off her furniture for this move to Norway, but Josephine and Oluf hung on to their rental property, a duplex and small cottage, in Millville because their plan had always been to return to America after a visit.

Their oldest son Tony had been back and forth and even lived out west in Chicago for a time, but was now back living in Christiana running a successful business selling coal to households there. Unfortunately, rents were high in the city, and Trygve's mother Inge, who they were, after all, trying to comfort, lived in Halden, a two-hour train ride south. So, Valle and the grandchildren would live in Halden in Trygve's family's old summer hut while Trygve would live and work with his brother-in-law in the city. Trygve would take the train back to Halden and his wife and family on the weekends.

At arrival, the SS Bergensfyord was greeted with fanfare and relief at the port of Christiana. After their prolonged and harrowing voyage, the family immediately boarded the train to Halden, to be reunited with Inge and relatives there. Valle watched the skyline of her beloved city disappear. Ships lined the port and stood at attention by the wharfs. Colorful boats bobbed with their white masts swaying back and forth. The neat lines of buildings and houses got smaller and disappeared. She watched out the window as the train headed toward Halden south of Christiana on the Tiste River and the border with Sweden.

~

Trygve soon returned to Christiana with Valle's parents to begin his new job selling and delivering coal with his brother-in-law to begin making some money. Valle lived with relatives she barely knew in an unfamiliar town, in a rugged summer hut, not far from her in-law's home, after more than a decade of living in America. Valle's memories of Norway were of Christiana and from childhood.

Valle was lonely and bored in this new place, surrounded by relatives she had never known. However, Inge took great delight in her beautiful grandchildren, praising Valle and adoring the children. But Inge had two of her own younger children still at home to keep her busy. And of course, all the family in Halden continued mourning the loss of their darling Soveig. And Valle had forgotten how light it was all day in summer when the sun barely set. The children could not sleep and the entire family was constantly sleep deprived and cranky.

Then there was food. Both Valle and Trygve were thrilled with the abundance, once again, of their beloved Norwegian cheeses. The supply of fresh fish and seafood was welcome. But, living in Catholic neighborhoods in Massachusetts meant that there was always a weekly peddler with fresh fish from Boston. Here at her mother-in-law's there was no good Georgia peach readily available. Valle mistakenly thought that her relatives would be interested in American food and once explained how she had learned to make a delicious clam chowder with tomatoes, bacon, and potatoes. There was a moment of silence in the room as her cousins contemplated this combination.

One of them finally said, "Well, I suppose if there is nothing else to eat," shrugged and changed the subject.

Homesick one day, Valle began reminiscing about the different boiled dinners she and her mother had learned to make in America. There was a variety of food available at the A&P and their Polish neighbors had shown her how to cook kielbasa and the Irish neighbors their version of corned beef. Her father-in-law had been in the room and he turned, aghast,

"Catholics? You learned to cook like Catholics? What's wrong with lupskous?"

Valle, remembering the professional medical staff at St. Vincent Hospital, who had saved Trygve's life, willed her mouth shut, lips tight, and did not reply.

The Svendsen family in Halden were members of the Methodist Church which was right down the street from their house. Valle found a comfortable place among the faithful here. Although she had childhood memories of Sunday services in the imposing Trinity Church in Christiana, with its classic majesty and lofty ceilings, Valle had become used to a more relaxed style of worship in the evangelical churches in America. The solemn liturgy of the Lutheran worship, although beautiful, had seemed empty compared to the powerful teaching of pastors in these new churches. Although the beauty of the building itself inspired reverence for the Almighty, Valle had become accustomed to finding God less in the brilliance of sun shining through the deep reds and blues of stained glass, and more in Bible reading and study. Organ music may soar to the lofty ceilings of the Lutheran Church, but Valle was now far more comfortable with lively guitars and violins and the harmony of rounds. And then there was Harriet.

Harriet initially exuberantly entered the adventure of school in Norway only to find school very different from what she had experienced in Millville. Harriet had begun going to school in America the year before back in Millville. The Blackstone River Valley there in New England was thriving with factories and immigrants pouring into the area filling the many jobs created. Towns struggled to keep up with needed classrooms and new teachers as the population, and the population of children not speaking English, increased.

Harriet's first year of school in America had been in a portable classroom with a young, new teacher who motivated the students by offering them the privilege of combing her hair for her before her boyfriend stopped by at the end of each day, if they were good. So besides learning the alphabet and singing patriotic songs, the girls were all learning how to French braid. If the boys misbehaved, they were sent to a corner to quietly play marbles.

The teacher in Norway sat in her chair above the class on a stage, her hair pulled back tight in a bun, spectacles perched on her nose. The teacher could not pronounce 'Harriet', and so used her middle name, Ruth, which she could not pronounce either. "Root Lee!, Root Lee!" was what Harriet heard all day.

In America, the children had recited their ABCs, sang patriotic songs, and taught each other to say things like 'I farted' and 'You poopy face' in Polish, Italian, Finnish, and many other languages. So Harriet was not used to Norwegian ways. She liked telling stories about America, some of which may have been exaggerated. Used to going to school and playing with a pack of boisterous kids from many countries, Harriet held her own when other children teased her for her American ways.

"Do you want to see something else American?" she coyly asked. Then she would put up her dukes like a prize fighter or pound them with snowballs. One day Harriet got homesick and just walked home in the middle of the day. The next afternoon the teacher cornered Valle as the children were being dismissed.

"Mrs. Lee, Mrs. Lee. I need to discuss your daughter's behavior in school."

"I am so glad to have the chance to talk to you. Harriet, that is Harriet Ruth, has herself told me she sometimes feels…"

"Root has not yet, I think, adjusted to school life in Norway." the teacher interrupted Valle. "We have an expectation of a certain decorum, a certain attitude of obedience and order that seems to be missing with your daughter. I am talking about respect." The teacher looked over her glasses at Valle. Valle opened her mouth to speak but the teacher continued, "I do hope you and your husband can convince your daughter to obey the rules. She seems to take delight in instigating social chatter at the most inopportune times. Training. Training is missing. Perhaps her good Norwegian grandfather, Mr. Hermann Svendsen can be of some help to those who have been influenced by destructive attitudes and succumbed to more modern distortions of respect and obedience," she sucked in a breath as Valle stood with her mouth open and who for once was speechless in her own native language.

Before Valle could respond the teacher added one passing word. "Training, training, Mrs. Lee. You must train your Root to obey."

Her independent and impish nature was not winning her any favor or friends in her new school. Valle was perplexed. Harriet had never had problems before. In fact, her daughter seemed very bright and was beginning piano lessons from her grandmother and showing some progress and interest. Reluctantly, Valle spoke to her in-laws about the conversation. Of course Inge already assumed Harriet was preparing for the life of a concert pianist. Hermann sat his granddaughter down for a talk.

"So, Harriet, my darling granddaughter, what is this I hear about you talking in class and maybe not paying attention to the teacher?"

"Oh, Far, I am so happy living here with you. You are my favorite Far in all the world."

"Thank you dear, but what about school? What about the teacher? Do you listen to the teacher?"

"Oh school is very good. The teacher is very good. The teacher talks all the time. She doesn't know how to sing. But she knows how to talk. We all listen to her. That is what we do all day. We listen to the teacher. She is very good at giving directions."

"So my Harriet, you must listen to the teacher and follow her instructions."

"Oh, yes! I will listen to the teacher, Far. And I will tell her that you told me to. Far, can I sing you a song?"

The grandparents came to Valle and said that they thought Harriet was precocious and everything was fine. Hermann thought her a perfect little girl. Perhaps she just needed a little more time to adjust.

After weeks of her mother giving her lectures, Harriet had a change of heart and decided to take things in her own hands to make friends. Harriet asked the teacher's permission and, in front of the entire class, invited all the children to her house the next day after school for her birthday party. So, the next day all the children strode with excitement to Harriet's after school. Of course, it was not her birthday and Harriet's mother and grandmother knew nothing about this party. Valle looked out and saw all these children playing in the yard. There were children hiding behind bushes and running around the house. Valle shooed them all home. Valle was back for a conference with the first-grade teacher about the behavior of this wayward American child. Later in life, Harriet, with a sly smile and a twinkle in her eye, would refer to first grade in Norway as her "year studying abroad".

Christmas Eve Halden

The children loved their grandparents. Trygve's younger siblings enjoyed playing with the children. Hoping to help Inge get through this difficult first Christmas without Solveig, Valle and the children helped Inge make the many Christmas cookies needed for such a large family. Inge enjoyed teaching Harriet piano and all the children their Christmas carols.

At the Christmas Eve services at church, Hermann walked around carrying Dorothy, his youngest granddaughter, her blonde curls tied back with red ribbon. Hermann proudly showed her off to his friends, while his wife and Valle readied Harriet for her first solo performance. With Inge at the piano, Harriet was thrilled to stand in front of the church and sing in her sweet soprano voice, "Maria Syng for Jesus Barnet". The service continued with the Christmas story read and more carols, ending with a lyrical acapella "Silent Night". The church bells rang as they headed up the street for home, the snow crunching under their feet, the churchgoers all wishing each other happy Christmas wishes, as they headed for their Christmas Eve meal and celebration. The family hungrily sat down to a feast of lutefisk, meat balls, pork loin served with peas and potatoes, pickled cabbage and sweet breads smeared with butter.

The children expected Julenissen to arrive any time. But first they all held hands and danced around the Christmas tree singing the traditional "I Am So Happy Every Christmas Eve." They sang the even more joyous, "O Jul Men Din Glede" skipping around the tree and singing the refrain again and again, "We clap our hands, we sing and we laugh, so happy we are, so happy we are." Then bang, bang at the door. The children squealed with delight as Grandpa Hermann opened the door and who should be there but Julenissen dressed in his red coat, hat and a funny-looking white beard. Sounding and looking a lot like great uncle Tobias, he stepped in and looked around, "Are there any good boys and girls here?" Dorothy, the youngest, wailed and ran to Valle, and the other children laughed and jumped.

"Let's see what I have in here." With great gusto, he pulled out gifts one at a time. Sophia, who was older, got a new hair ribbon and barrette, Fritjolf a pocketknife, Harriet a rag doll dressed in pink, David a toy cart, and Dorothy who refused to get near the scary man, a wooden pull duck. Next the Julenissan pulled out a big box of chocolates. "Ho, ho, and we now all get a piece of chocolate."

"Oh wait, you forgot Solveig." Inge reached for a small tissue wrapped package above the fireplace. "I made this for Solveig. Where is Solveig?" The grieving mother and grandmother looked around at the quiet adults. The room was suddenly solemn. "Where's Solveig? We cannot forget Solveig."

"Where's Solveig?" Inga's voice was louder, sharper.

"Inge, dear, we all miss Solveig. So, so dear of you to make her something, for her memory. So kind of you..."

"Where's Solveig?" her eyes searched frantically around the room.

And then Inge ran out the door, screaming "Solveig, Solveig, where are you..?" as her husband took off after her down the street. "Solveig, Solveig," Inge's voice echoed in the cold night. In the dark, in the snow, Inge did not get far before she tripped and landed in a drift by the side of the road... Trygve ran after them. Hermann kneeled beside her.

"Let me help you up. Did you hurt yourself? Oh, Inge..."

She got to her feet and looked wildly at her husband and son, tears streaming down their faces, "Where's Solveig?"

"Inge dear, we all miss Solveig, Solveig, Solveig, she's with Jesus Inge, she's in heaven with Jesus."

"Well, Jesus can't have her. I want her!" Inge screamed, pounding her chest. "I want her. I want her here. I want Solveig to walk through that door." She pointed back toward the house. "I want Solveig with me." And she whimpered, "Not Jesus, Jesus can't have her."

"I know, Inge. It's alright, it's alright to be

mad, mad at God. God can take our anger. He knows. He understands."

She tore open the package and held up a lace trimmed handkerchief, shaking it in the air. "See this? I made this for her. For Solveig. I want Solveig to be here. I want to give her her gift."

"Oh Inge, dear. You can be angry with God. He understands. That's why we celebrate tonight. Right? Inge, dear. Jesus came as an infant. Jesus came and lived with us. He understands."

"I don't want Him to understand. I want Solveig back." She let out a plaintiff moan, sounding like an injured animal.

Inge fell into her husbands' arms and sobbed. Trygve draped his coat over her back. When Inge calmed down a little, she stepped back and wiped her eyes with the handkerchief, and in a small voice asked,

"I want Solveig. My life will never be the same, will it?"

"No, dear, no. Your life, our lives, will never be the same. But look, dear," he pointed her back to the house, with candles glowing in the windows, "Look, the children are there at the door waiting for us. They will worry. We must go back. Let's go back, Inge."

Inge sighed and took her husband's arm. The father, son, and mother shuffled through the snow to the warmth of the house and the Christmas Eve celebration.

Coal

While Valle was struggling to fit in, her husband was attempting to grow his business and there was the hope that the family could all soon be together in Christiana. The Norwegian economy continued suffering from high unemployment and the country was just getting over a national workers strike. The price of coal had recently dropped, and Tony had sold this as an opportunity for growth, as he said more people would now use coal and they could expand the business. Trygve was beginning to realize this would be difficult. Expenses were mounting for the business.

Coal was sold by weight or the bucket. For each household, the coal man would fill each skuttle and charge a set amount per bucket. Trygve was an honest businessman who needed to expand his business if he was to bring his family to live with him in Christiana. Tony was happy that his brother-in-law was ambitious and building his route until Tony realized that he was losing his customers to his own brother-in-law and partner.

Trygve was not a natural salesman and was more accustomed to working in factories and running machinery than dealing with customers. However, if he wanted to get his family living together in one spot again, he needed to make this venture succeed. Trygve dug deep in his soul to tap inner resources he never knew he had to keep and increase his customers. Neither being too hot or cold, physically tired or dirty, or frustrated with what he thought was a piece of junk for a truck, none of these challenges were as difficult for him as dealing with his business partner and customers. Trygve exhausted every effort to build his business and could only hope that Tony was doing the same.

Tony met Trygve at the end of a long day with a question that sounded more like an accusation.

"Trygve, I thought we were supposed to be partners and work as one business?" Pausing, Trygve looked over at his brother in law's tense face and wondered what had aggravated him now.

"What are you talking about? What is your problem now?"

"My problem? My problem?! I lost another customer today. You know who to? To you! You and your crazy ways. You are so stubborn. I told you how to measure the coal in the skuttle." Tony was becoming uncharacteristically animated, acting out his frustration. "I told you. You must fill the bucket and then use the stick to level the amount. Level it! Like this. You! You want to fill a pail to overflowing. Heap in as much as you can fit. Just so you can get more customers."

"So, do you know what has happened? Oh, you think you are so smart, such a smart American businessman. What do the customers get? Instead of buying one pail of coal from our business. OUR business, they buy more coal for the same price from you. But the cost of hiring out these barges is going up. Gasoline is going up. Food prices are going up. But no, you are selling more coal for less. These housewives are buying just a skuttle full of coal at a time but we need every customer."

Trygve stood arms crossed and silent. Tony took a breath and continued, "And don't carry coal upstairs for the ladies. I'm not lugging coal into apartments or upstairs." Tony headed for the trolley in a huff. Trygve decided to walk.

The coal delivery business was not making money. Barely able to pay their creditors and keep up with costs, both men were exhausted at the end of the day and just as broke as they were the day before. Trygve had walked the streets of the city searching for an apartment suitable for a family with three active little ones. He knew his wife was eager to be united and living under one roof in the city but he could not afford the rent. In Halden the children had fields and parks and family around. Trygve did not want to lie but did not know how to tell his wife how dire their circumstances were.

In Halden, Valle was by now alone. Both of her parents had returned to America and back to their home in Millville. Oluf was back in Millville making boots, and making money, and Josephine was helping with grandchildren there. Valle, tired of being separated from her husband, finally decided they had to face the truth. She wrote a short letter to her husband in Christiana, admitting maybe this was not working and that she wanted to return to America. What did he think?

Trygve opened and read the letter and immediately set off for the shipping office to book passage back to America.

Hudson

The Lee family returned to Millville and the familiar community there. But job opportunities were a little tighter than expected back now in America. Trygve heard that the Firestone Rubber and Tire Company was hiring in Hudson and so he ended up, once again, separated from the family, living in Hudson during the week. This time Trygve stayed in a boarding house and commuted weekends home to his family with others from the area who were working at the factories in Hudson. Prospects and pay were better in Hudson than Millville and soon the Lee family moved to the bustling factory town in central Massachusetts.

Valle had to move miles from her parents and family, but after the arrangement in Norway, she was happy to keep her own family together. And her parents were not that far away. But now the Lees would not be renting from or living with relatives. Housing was tight and expensive, and the only apartment they could find in Hudson was in the back of a store on the corner of Apsley Street. This apartment had 2 bedrooms, a kitchen with running water and an indoor flush toilet, which was something new for the family. Having the store right there made picking up groceries convenient.

Although there were not many Scandinavians in town, the Lees found a few friends. There was at least one large Swedish family, the Ericksons who they were friends with and there was a Methodist Church right down the street with those oh, so familiar hymns and shared faith.

On Friday evenings and Saturdays everyone in town dressed up and walked up and down Main Street to shop. Dry goods and clothing stores flourished where customers could put their new coat, hat, or Victrola on layaway to pay off weekly. The jewelry stores also carried the latest records and sheet music. There were two theaters, not that the Lees would frequent such a worldly venue. The Elm Street Theater even offered live Amatuer Acts for 30 cents. Buses took you everywhere and at the train depot on lower Main Street there was regular service to Boston or Worcester, and the world beyond.

The children went to school. Valle gathered all the emotional strength she could and applied for a job at Firestone. She had worked in the factories of Millville before she was married and knew what awaited her on the job in a factory but she did not want to, once again, disrupt her family. Suddenly, Valle felt that the family had moved too frequently. The family needed stability. All three children were now in school and needed her less. She could give Harriet the key and the children could let themselves in after school. Harriet and David could even stop by and pick up the milk or bread at the store.

What could go wrong?

Dorothy, the youngest, stayed for lunch at her elementary school but the older two walked home from Harriman School for lunch every day. Harriet was happier in school back in America but grew tired of the same old thing for lunch, particularly when they were practically living in a store full of tempting choices. Every day she would come home to butter dry bread and assemble the potato sandwiches for her and her brother. If they were lucky, once and awhile there would be buttered bread with cheese. Not only did she have to eat the boring lunch but she had to bear the complaining of her siblings, as if she was responsible for the bland meals. David and Dorothy whined and complained at her for the endless potato sandwiches and boiled hot dogs for dinner. It was so unfair. One potato sandwich too many, and Harriet entered the store to consider her lunch alternatives.

"Hello Harriet, what can I get you? Are you out of milk?"

"Oh, no, it's the ..." Harriet hesitated as she took in the vast volume of food choices, the lunch meats, white bread, cheeses and delights like jam, and yummy Norwegian sardines or tins of peaches, all of which would have been delicious for lunch.

"My mother wanted me to buy that." Harriet pointed.

"This? Which one, the white cake or the chocolate cake?" Mr. McCarthy queried.

"The chocolate."

"Are you sure that your mother wants you to

buy this whole chocolate cake?"

"Yes, I am to bring it to school today."

"OK, I'll put it on your bill."

Harriet carefully carried her treasure back to the apartment where David waited for his lunch.

"Harriet what is that? What have you got there?"

"I bought us lunch," as she smiled as she unveiled the chocolate feast.

"Are you crazy? What have you done? How are you going to keep this secret?"

"We are going to have all the chocolate cake we want for lunch and then I'll bring the rest to school," she replied as she began slicing the cake.

"We are going to get into so much trouble. Oh, I don't think this is a good idea," his voice got softer and softer. He picked up his fork and dug in.

David helped her devour a good portion of the cake. When it was time to return to school, Harriet cleaned up and brought the rest of the cake with her to share with her classmates before they went into class.

That evening as the children were sitting at the table and Valle was preparing dinner, Trygve arrived home and opened the door and surveyed his children.

"Well, Harriet, do you have anything to tell me, your father, about your day at school today? Or maybe about your lunch today?"

David began to cry. Harriet was silent. Then she burst into a loud wail.

Valle turned around, "What is going on?"

"Well, I think Harriet is the one who should tell

us. Harriet. Tell your mother what you did at lunch today."

"I am sorry, Pa, I couldn't help it."

"You couldn't help it? What is that supposed to mean?"

"The cake looked so good. And I knew that David didn't want a sandwich. I had to get the cake for David."

"You got a cake for David?" Valle was confused.

"Yes, your daughter bought an entire chocolate cake for lunch today from the store."

Dorothy stood up, "What? Did you save any for me? Do I get some chocolate cake? Where is my cake?"

"Harriet, where is the cake?" Valle asked.

"We ate about half of it for lunch and I brought the rest to school, and we ate it on the playground before school. There is no more cake left."

Dorothy picked up a nearby doll and whacked her sister in the back. "You didn't save any cake for me?"

"Don't hit your sister."

"Do you know how much that cake cost? I have to pay for that cake."

"Pa, are you going to buy me any cake? I want a piece of chocolate cake. They both got huge pieces of chocolate cake!"

"No one is getting any more chocolate cake. The point is Harriet shouldn't have bought the cake to begin with."

Dorothy threw herself on the floor kicking the table and floor. "It's not fair. I want chocolate cake too. It's not fair. They got cake." Harriet sat silent and sullen, and David wept.

Trygve and Valle looked at each other and shook their heads.

~

The three-room apartment was cramped and Mr. McCarthy the landlord and store owner was increasingly difficult to live with, particularly after the chocolate cake incident. Finally, Trygve read an ad for a second-floor apartment available on nearby Butman Street. Valle and Trygve had some late-night discussions and prayer concerning the budget. But since this apartment was larger, Trygve and Valle offered boarding to her brother who was looking for work. With a boarder paying rent, Valle would be able to stay home. The Lee family moved into the three-bedroom apartment and Uncle Hans came to board with them Monday through Friday since he was working as a bookkeeper at the factory.

On moving day, the three children were ushered into the bathroom in their new home to behold the splendors of a modern apartment. Not only was there a beautiful porcelain flush toilet, but a gleaming white claw foot tub. No more baths in a tub in the kitchen on Saturday night for the Lee family. Admiring the luxurious conveniences, the oil stove and shiny wood floors and even an enclosed front porch off the living room, the Lee family had reason to feel a sense of satisfaction. Hot water, an oil stove, electricity, and a tub; the Lees had finally arrived. And Valle would no longer work.

Valle felt a sense of relief tinged with concern. She knew that money would be tight. But both Trygve and Valle put their faith in the hands of God. He would always provide, not money floating down from heaven or celestial gifts, but a way, a job, a means to work. So, for now her brother would pay them board and the family could make ends meet. The schools were good, the work plentiful, and Harriet had a piano teacher.

There was plenty of room for a piano in their new apartment. Valle found a secondhand piano advertised in the paper and asked around for a good piano teacher. Uncomfortable and shy about her English, she had practiced with Harriet on how to walk to the teacher's home and sent Harriet on to the first lesson by herself. Valle had learned to take Harriet's spirited temperament and give her an outlet for all her energy. Being able to take on this responsibility and have the attention of a piano teacher all to herself was more than enough motivation for Harriet to obey her mother's instructions.

"Here is the money. Now, don't lose it. Put it in your pocket." Harriet was thrilled with the responsibility and opportunity to go somewhere by herself.

"Now, Harriet, when you get there, be polite but ask the teacher where she studied music. If she says the Boston Conservatory, then go ahead and have the lesson." Mrs. Wheeler was indeed a graduate of the conservatory and thus Harriet's musical education proceeded.

Then, Uncle Hans found better employment

back in his hometown and would no longer be boarding with them. Valle and Trygve were concerned. Valle did not want to go back to working in the factory. Trygve was tired of paying rent and wanted to buy a house.

The immediate problem could be solved with another boarder. But who? Hans was a family member but allowing a complete stranger into your home seemed mildly reckless. Valle and Trygve discussed how they could manage a stranger boarding with them. They decided they could rent the enclosed front porch out as a bedroom. Then the family's bedrooms were in the rear of the house. The many workers in town had ample available meals at the company boarding house. The Lees could rent the front room for less than a room boarding at the factory-run boarding house, and Valle could stay home. With prayer and trepidation, Valle put out an ad. After all, the Lees only needed to find someone that could be trusted with a key.

The Boarder

And so one cool Sunday evening in the fall, as the light faded, Harriet and David hid in bushes along the sidewalk with a couple of David's friends to watch the boarder come to the Lee's for the week.

"He should be coming soon. He usually comes about this time." David whispered a little loudly to his impatient buddies as they all peered through the bushes down the street, hoping to catch sight of the approaching man.

"Are you sure he's from Chicago? Why would anyone from Chicago move here?"

"Yes," Harriet offered firmly. "He had to leave Chicago and hide here in a small town far from the mob bosses. The mob bosses would kill him. They'd shoot him dead.' She added with emphasis to convey the seriousness of this dire situation to her doubting neighbors.

"Why would they kill him?"

"Because he isn't a bootlegger anymore. Or selling whiskey. Or something,"

"What is a bootlegger?"

"Why," Harriet pronounced confidently,

"Everyone knows a bootlegger is a rum runner."

"Ohh," They all nodded in agreement, unwilling to appear ignorant.

"Here he comes," whispered David excitedly.

Mr. McKinney sauntered around the corner onto Butman Street with a small black satchel in one hand and newspapers under his arm, only thinking of the work week ahead of him. He took the train from Cambridge every week to Hudson to board with the Lees and work at the Apsley Rubber Factory, but only until he could find a job closer to Boston. There was a waiting list for beds at the factory owned boarding house and he was happy to find a room to rent with a family. Of course Trygve was happy to have someone else around who read the paper and was up for a good, well informed discussion.

When Valle Lee had shown him the room and interviewed him, he had been honest about his past. He indeed had been a 'rum runner' in Illinois, piloting boats full of good whiskey across the Great Lakes from Canada for consumption in Chicago. But after spending a couple of months in jail, he was done with bootlegging of any kind. Mr. McKinney found a sympathetic ear with his new landlady. Valle decided to trust him because he was honest and forthright. And what good Christian lady could not sympathize with a changed life? So indeed, a former rum runner and bootlegger climbed the back stairs to the Lees flat and poked his head into the kitchen. There he gave Trygve the newspapers, took a seat, and chatted with him, accepting a piece of pound cake from Valle before heading to his room at the front of the apartment.

Mr. McKinney was totally unaware that he was the object of such interest. David's friends however, were not impressed.

"He doesn't look so different," they grumbled.

"That is because he is in hiding. He can't LOOK like he is from Chicago or they would find him," Harriet retorted.

Hudson was a thriving community. Main Street was alive with people shopping for necessities or just out for a stroll. Customers might be entertained by demonstrations of the latest gas stoves or a Victrola that comes with easy terms all while the newest Ford or roadster whizzed by. Trygve and Valle, impressed by the demonstration at Robinsons Hardware Store of the many attachments for the latest treadle Singer Sewing Machine, purchased the latest oak cabinet model.

However, Trgve was frustrated.

Trgve explored the various neighborhoods looking for a house or land he could afford to buy. Often after Sunday morning services at the Hudson Methodist Church, the family could be found walking up and down streets looking at houses, lots, or checking out neighborhoods. Trygve searched out advertised land and houses for sale or any rumor he had heard of some house, lot, or fixer upper someone might want to get rid of. There were house lots advertised for seven hundred dollars. But even if he saved up the money, where would they live while they built a house? The family kept walking.

Then at work, Trygve met a man from Nova Scotia who owned land close to Hudson but over the line in the more rural town of Bolton. He wanted to sell the property and move back to Nova Scotia but was having trouble selling the nearly ten acres with a couple of structures. There was a garage and house that was maybe not habitable. Currently there were chickens living in the house. Trygve was interested.

The Bank

"Mr. Lee, the bank cannot give you a mortgage on this property. You have no credit, no..."

"But please, I have these references...my bank statement, a letter from the foreman..."

But the banker pushed the papers back to him. The banker stood up and pushed his chair back, shaking his head. "Mr. Lee, I am sorry. And the property, the property is not an investment the bank wants to make."

Trygve stood up too. He leaned forward slightly, eyeball to eyeball to the banker across the desk. In a tight voice, barely controlling his anger, "My money is as good as anyone else's." The two men held their stance for a long moment. Then Trygve took his letters and papers and walked out of the bank.

Christian Trygve Lee was confused. Trygve had been to banks in Clinton, Hudson and now Marlborough. No bank would give him a mortgage at a time in 1925 when mortgage rates had fallen and the number of home mortgages being written had tripled. Other men he worked with at the

Firestone Rubber Company factory were moving into new homes; yet as a tool maker who kept those machines running, he made a higher wage and still could not get a loan. Trygve may have been a skilled factory worker, but he was still an immigrant. He now knew there would be no bank loan for him and his family.

Why did the banks consider the property a poor investment? He was flabbergasted. When a coworker, knowing Trygve was looking for property, told him about this ten-acre lot on the market, Trygve was immediately interested. The house on the property, uninhabited for years, he knew was of little value and needed an enormous amount of work, but Trygve was confident he could rebuild the house. There were also two other buildings, a large garage and smaller shed. But the real value was the land; ten acres of land in South Bolton, on the Hudson, Berlin, and Bolton town lines, very near the train depot. Just a short walk and you could catch the train to Boston or a bus to Hudson or Worcester. In fact, because this bucolic, forested neighborhood was an easy commute directly to Boston, some of the homes there were summer residences of city families.

The entire lot was on higher ground than the nearby brook and Hog Swamp right across the street. The lot boasted a lovely pine grove with a old road that led into the surrounding woods. The ancient glaciers that had once covered New England had also left three gifts on the land. One gift, a solitary gray boulder, taller than a person, sat inexplicably alone in the backyard. Then past the pine grove and down a small hill, was a deposit of clean, almost beach-like sand and gravel, perfect for mixing cement. Next to the house and near the road, was a large flat area Trygve had eyed for a garden. This field had a few trees that would need uprooting to make enough room and sunshine for a good garden. Also in that field and future garden was the glacier's third gift: a never-ending supply of stones and rocks.

Trygve was convinced there was value in the land. One banker had tried to suggest that Trygve might have better luck getting a loan on a more expensive new home like the many that were being built on small lots and quickly selling closer to town. But a Norwegian knew there was value in land. You could always build a house; you could not build land. And he was not interested in a larger loan. How could anyone think these ten acres were not a great investment?

So with disappointment and reluctance, Trygve went home to his wife, and discussed, again, the alternate plan. They would drive after church to her brother's and borrow the money from him. Hans Anderson was a bookkeeper and accountant who worked in a nearby town. Even though Hans also had a family and young child, he had made money investing in the stock market and had already eagerly offered to lend Trygve money to buy a house. Trygve wrote up an agreement offering to pay Hans the same rate of return as he would have to the bank.

The Lee family would have their valuable land even if the banks were foolish.

PLENTEOUS GRACE

The House

Trygve Lee was vindicated. After years of hard work, saving money and providing for his family; he now owned land. The house was small, basic, and previously inhabited by chickens. There was a garage in the rear of the home and also a small shed-like structure. The family would have a roof over their heads, but the value of the property was not in the buildings.

A small grove of pine trees, a flat field for a garden, real land, this is the value. He could walk around the perimeter, let the sand run through his fingers, or dig in the dirt. His dirt. His sand. His boundary. He owed the mortgage but there would be no more rent for him to pay. His earthly treasure would be invested in his own soil for his, and his family's future.

But the calming elation of owning land was curbed by urgent needs. The truck transporting their belongings, the piano and a few large pieces of furniture, was barely off the dead end street when Trygve had his wife and children stand off to one side as he climbed up a ladder and onto the roof. He did not trust the construction of this house he had just purchased. He shimmied across the peak of the roof to the stone chimney on the side of the house and gave the stone chimney a shove with the bottom of his foot. A column of white dust from the dried-out mortar circled in the spring breeze as the entire chimney fell to the ground in a noisy clumsy pile of rocks and dust. The condition of the house was just as he had assessed. Trygve waved down at his wife and children looking up at him, their mouths opened aghast.

"The foundation is bad too. I'm going to have to rebuild all the basement walls."

The two-story house was small. There was an open living and dining area with a small kitchen at the back of the house with just room for the stove and a small kitchen table. A side open staircase in the living room led to a large hall and two small bedrooms. There was plenty of room for David to have a cot in the hall and the girls to share one of the rooms now that the chickens were out of there. Trygve and Valle had already discussed the need to extend the back entrance enclosing a porch and add room for a tub to the bathroom there. They also had their eye on a new oil stove for the kitchen. Trygve, however, was more anxious to set a firm foundation and prepare the house for the coming of winter.

Trygve rented industrial size jacks and had the entire house jacked up. The family walked in and out of the house on planks while Trygve dug footings and built forms for the foundation walls. The cement truck arrived, poured the concrete, and finished up the job. With firm walls and a new secure chimney, the house was back on its own foundation, ready for the most modern coal burning furnace Trygve could buy. Of course, he would first have to plumb the house for steam heat. To save money, Trygve found secondhand radiators in good condition but in a variety of colors and styles. A long white ornate radiator heated the living room and shorter, stubbier ones upstairs would whistle and clank in other rooms through the coming winter months.

Trygve was exhausted with the constant physical work. Valle was pleased to be living on their own property but finding life in the country a change and challenge. There was no more walking around Main Street on a Saturday, or even walking to church services. Instead, the family could squeeze into the Model T Ford they now owned. The old ice box refrigerator leaked, and the stove cooked unevenly. No gleaming white clawfoot tub or electric lighting here in rural Bolton like there had been in their apartment on Butman Street. But the children seemed to have adjusted quickly. Dorothy had a new friend to play with, David found friends in the neighborhood, and Harriet continued her piano lessons. Valle was hopeful that this new neighborhood would bring some peace and stability into their lives.

The Neighborhood

Sitting right next to the house on a hill next to them was a small cottage with a front porch overlooking their yard. Their neighbor, John Fahey hailed from Nova Scotia and lived with his much younger wife Clara and his granddaughter Mary and his older disabled daughter Gladys. John was a tall skinny gray headed man who also worked in a factory in Hudson. John's daughter Gladys had club feet and hands and rarely left the house but liked to sit by the window with scissors and cut up paper. Gladys did not speak, although she could communicate her enthusiasm or dismay with guttural vocalizations and gestures, waving to all and keeping watch over the small neighborhood from her perch there by the window.

Clara was much younger than her husband and had no other children of her own. Her dark hair was usually tied up in a bun. Every morning Clara would leave to catch the bus for her housekeeping work in town, smoking her pipe as she left the house. In an attempt to hide her smoking from her new neighbors, she held her parasol off to the side, covering her head, even as the smoke rose over the circle of protection.

John Fahey was thin, stooped over with gray hair. John had a large family from his first marriage and Mary was one of his grandchildren. Mary's parents and multiple siblings lived in town while Mary kept her grandparents company in their home in the country a few miles down the road.

The Fahey family fairly filled this house to overflowing when they all came over for a visit. On warm summer nights, Clara would strum her zither and lead the family in song as they sipped their moonshine.

That first summer, the Lee family, usually exhausted from their labors, would spend evening in their home listening to the plaintiff songs their neighbor plucked on her instrument. Clara sang as she became increasingly relaxed and melodious through the evening. She pulled from her large repertoire of hymns or drinking and folk songs at her fingertips.

Mary and Dorothy would be in the same grade at school that next year so Dorothy had a built-in best friend to play with. The two were together most days and if they were not wandering in the woods, they could often be found making doll furniture with sticks and old boxes. Oatmeal containers became decorated cradles when cut in half and scraps of cloth and left over wallpaper became doll clothing. Mary helped keep an eye on Gladys and both girls helped keep Gladys supplied with old papers and newspapers to cut up.

The nearby depot gave the rural neighborhood access to transportation and provided income for a

middle-aged widow. Mrs. McCarthy who lived
nearby the depot and just over the Berlin town line
baked bread and goods for a restaurant in Hudson.
The daily train run provided transportation for her
goods. Every morning she could be seen bringing
her boxes of parker rolls to the train as it pulled in
from Worcester on its way to the next stop, Hudson,
and eventually Boston. But the baked goods only
rode for one stop and there in lower Main Street in
Hudson by the depot the local diner would pick
their delivery. Mrs. McCarthy was the first one in
the area to get a telephone installed and her door
was always open. There in her kitchen neighbors
could leave a coin and make a needed telephone call
if they knew anyone who had a telephone
themselves.

The summer days went quickly. Just getting the
house   cleaned   and   habitable   had   been
overwhelming. Somehow, with David's help, there
was a small vegetable garden. The rooms had been
swept and cleaned. The windows were filmy and
needed to be washed; the kitchen cleaned and
organized. The ice box was old and leaked and this
had been a hot summer.   On some nights the
upstairs had been so hot that Trygve and Valle had
pulled the mattresses downstairs and the family had
camped out in the living room which was cooler
than upstairs. Trygve had installed screen doors and
so there was at least some air circulation.

The children soon heard that the local woods
was full of blueberry bushes. Valle and the children
headed out with buckets, their necks covered in
kerchiefs, long sleeves and long pants covering as

much as possible to protect from the mosquitoes. The caravan headed through the pine trees and into the woods on the cart road that led who knows where but ended at the top of a hill. Then they headed down to lower land near a boggy area. Birds scattered to the trees as the noisy family approached. Blueberry bushes as tall as Valle went on as far as you could see in the thicket. Blueberries, sky blue to that sweet purple blue, hung in the ends, under the leaves, from the top to the lower branches. The family quickly got to work. Suddenly the woods were quiet, except for the occasional impatient complaint of the birds, or the children swatting one more mosquito. They moved through the thickets filling their buckets with berries. When there was no place for one more blueberry, they headed home.

Valle and Harriet got busy washing and sorting their berries. Trygve had saved the old oil stove from the kitchen and set it up in the shed for summer canning. So Valle, in the lightest of a summer shift, sweated in the shed, boiling batches of blueberries with just a little sugar. Then she sanitized the canning jars in boiling water before filling the steaming jars with the warm blueberry compote. Finally, the filled jars got a bath in boiling water for the final seal. The gleaming green canning jars sparkled as they cooled on shelves. Besides having heat, this winter the Lees would have blueberries.

David had returned to the blueberry bushes to pick more berries and found a market for his product. Down the street and across the railroad tracks Mrs. McCarthy, the neighborhood baker, was happy to purchase blueberries and later blackberries for pies. Mrs. McCarthy had a couple of stoves in her kitchen and baked the daily parker rolls but also baked pies and cookies for the diner there in Hudson. Every morning, her arms full of boxes of sweet-smelling rolls, she would meet the morning train from Worcester and hand off her bounty. Besides having access to her telephone, if the neighbors were lucky, there were leftover fluffy parker rolls for sale.

Surprise Visits

In the middle of a workday Valle was startled
by the sound and sight of cars coming up the street.
Parking right up near the house was their own Ford
but driven by some other man. Trygve slumped
over in the passenger seat of his own car while a
stranger drove it and another car followed. Valle
rushed out to meet them.

The driver came out. "Mrs. Lee, don't worry.
He's going to be OK. He cut himself and fainted."

"We'll help get him into the house."

One on either side of him, the men helped the
injured men up the steps and into the house, where
Trygve flopped down on the sofa.

"The nurse checked him out at the factory. He
didn't need stitches. She bandaged him up."

"He may have hit his head when he fainted, but
he came to right away."

"Thank you, so much, thank you." Valle said.

"Chris, we hope you're feeling better soon."

After they left to return to the factory, Trygve
held up his hand. His thumb was tightly bandaged.

"Look," he wiggled his bandaged thumb. "Oh
Valle, there was blood everywhere."

"Don't think about it now." Valle, who was accustomed to her husband's response to the sight of blood, learned long ago to be patient with her patient. "Let's get you comfortable. What do you want? Some water?"

"No, no, nothing. I feel so sick. Well, maybe a little coffee."

~

The rural neighborhood was small but not so remote that there were no visitors. Cars still shared the road with the occasional horse drawn peddler's wagon. These peddlers might sell vegetables, fruit, or dry goods. There was even a peddler who sharpened scissors. Valle could count on the fish peddler to have fresh fish every Friday so the Catholics could buy their fish for meatless Fridays. When the gypsies were in town, they made the rounds offering pony rides, photographs, and fortune telling. Insurance salesmen traveled their routes to collect payments and ice and coal were delivered. And of course, there were occasional visitors next door.

One day Mary came over to play with Dorothy and as usual the two ended up playing with their paper dolls.

"There aren't any more pictures to cut out in these magazines. Let's bring them over to Gladys so she can cut them up." Dorothy offered.

"Oh, no. Not now. I can't now. Do you see my uncle's car there? When he comes over, I have to leave. He's funny."

"How is he funny?"

Oh, he is funny alright. He doesn't want

anyone to know when he comes over. Well, I'm not supposed to talk about it. I am not supposed to go home when he is there. But I peek. But if you want, we could go and peek."

"Peek at what? See what?"

"Dorothy Lee, you must super promise three times that you'll never tell. But it is funny."

"I promise three times. I promise not to tell."

"We have to be really quiet."

"I can be quiet."

After more instructions from Mary, the two girls tiptoed toward the Fahey house. Slowly, very slowly, the girls approached the door. Mary carefully opened the door to avoid any squeaking. By now Gladys, who did not speak but could clearly communicate, was flapping her hands excitedly and putting her finger to lips to 'shhh...'' the girls. They motioned back to her and continued to tiptoe up the stairs. The girls could hear some muffled conversation and laughter and quietly, and excitedly, looked at each other and giggled. The pair continued up the stairs. Mary was expecting the bedroom door to be closed and the keyhole to be available, but the door was ajar and open. They would have to take a peek through the half open door. Dorothy followed Mary's example and they both leaned over and peeked into the bedroom.

A small gasp from the girls at the sight of Mrs. Boucher, Katy's mom from down the street, in her underwear, invoked a blood curdling scream from Mrs. Boucher. The girls turned and thundered down the stairs hearing curses from Mary's uncle, and then a loud thud, as he tripped on his pants, which were around his feet. More curses as he flew out of the house, pulling up his pants as he ran off the porch and down the hill, after the girls, and suddenly stopped in his tracks in front of Valle.

"Good day, Mr. Fahey. Are you looking for Mary? She is in the house. The girls are playing. No worry. They are fine."

"Thank you, Mrs. Lee," he managed as he tried to look casual and tuck his shirt in.

"And how is Mrs. Fahey? Am I right that you have a new baby?"

"No, that's my brother."

"Ah, well. It's so nice of you to come by in the middle of the week; and the middle of the day and look after Gladys. Tell your wife hello from me," she smiled and paused. "You might want to put a little ice on your lip."

Barefoot, he returned to the house. Valle proceeded to sit there on the front step with a large pot of green beans to snap. Slowly, she carefully snapped each bean. Snap. Plop. She took her time. Enjoyed the sunshine. When she had enough, she went in and ventured upstairs where she could still hear the girls giggling. From the window she watched his car finally leave in a cloud of dust. The girls, all this time, had been rolling around the room laughing so hard they were in tears. What a funny, surprising sight in the middle of the day.

The Visit

Valle was weeding her small garden plot. Trygve was at work. Dorothy and Mary were in the shade of the shed cutting up old Sears Roebuck Catalogs for their paper dolls, Harriet was busy inside and David was off somewhere. A shiny new Studebaker slowed on the road, backed up, and turned up the gravel road, kicking up stones, and then stopped at the end of their road. Valle nervously watched as two men in suits got out and went to the Fahey's. They pounded on the door. No answer and no movement. They knocked again and waited. Looking into windows, the two walked around the house and up a ways into the woods in back of the house.

The men approached Valle, who by now was herself headed into her house, 'Ma'am, is it Mrs. Lee? Good day, we were looking for your neighbor John Fahey, that is his house, is that correct?" He flashed an official looking paper for her to see.

"Yes."

"Ah, good. We wanted to talk to him. Have you seen him today at all?"

"No." Valle could respond truthfully.

"Seems he may know something about the illegal manufacture and sales of liquor or spirits." He wiped his brow.

"Do you know anything about the manufacturing of liquor here in the neighborhood?"

"No." Valle replied.

Valle remained silent and stoic. "Well Mrs. Lee, if you have anything you want to report or any problems at all, you can always contact the local police."

He tipped his hat, "We'll probably be back."

Gladys' head popped up in the window and she watched the shiny black car leave. Mary ran home. The Lee children raced to their mother with questions. "Who were those men?" "What did they want?" Valle was shaking but contained her emotions. "They were agents looking for Mary's grandfather. Prohibition agents. They just wanted to talk to our neighbor. We mind our business…"

"But, Ma, everyone knows that Mr. Fahey's still…." Valle clamped her hand over Dorothy's mouth. "Don't tell me. I do not need to know. I am not going to lie to anyone. If I don't know, I can't lie. But we are going to mind our own business. What our neighbors do is none of our business."

Letting go of her daughter, Valle added, "Now go. Enough of this. No more talk of this." And Valle fled to her room to recover and fall on her knees before God. How in the world would she and Trygve handle this situation? She, Valle Lee, had actually talked to enforcement agents. She was troubled and felt dirty.

Later that evening Valle was as casual as she

could be when repeating the story to her husband over dinner. The children added their descriptions of the men. Trgve had quietly chewed his food, listened, and said nothing. His silence was disconcerting, and the children were close mouthed about the whereabouts of the neighbor's still after the rebuke to Dorothy.

After dinner, Valle and Trygve walked out back to the privacy of the lush pine grove for a private conversation.

"Well, we have to mind our business," Trygve agreed with his wife. "We cannot be the cause of any more trouble for John. What he does is his business."

"But the children," Valle added, "If Dorothy knows where his still is, then everyone else, every child in this neighborhood, knows all about his still and his moonshine. What kind of example is this for our children?"

"We hate the sin and love the sinner, that's what," was Trygve's response. "That is all we can do. It is a fallen world and who knows what will happen to these prohibition laws."

They continued walking.

"But, Valle," He added, "I have another concern."

"What's that?"

"You, you my dear. School will start again, and you will be here by yourself, all day. I hate to think of you here all alone every day."

Valle was bemused, "Really? And what do you think is the answer? Maybe," she flirted, "You can get me a butler?"

"No, no Valle, I am thinking about something else. I am thinking of a dog, for protection."

She dropped her husband's hand, and took a couple steps back, away, and looked hard at her husband, "A dog? Husband, you want to get me a dog?"

Trygve knew when he was in trouble when she referred to him like that. "Valle, listen, there's nothing we can do about our neighbors. But a dog would be company for you…."

"A dog?" she interrupted "I spent days scraping chicken poop from that house and now maybe you think I need someone new to clean up after?"

The emotion of the day rolled out in a torrent of anger, "Maybe you think I can't take care of myself? Am I too helpless to know how to get help or too lonely for a friend, take a bus, or talk to a stranger, or speak English good enough? Will a dog speak English for me? Maybe I need another mouth to feed? More work to do?" She moved in close and with clenched teeth added, "I don't need more poop to clean up, from you or anyone." and marched back to the house.

Trygve slowly returned to the house. Perhaps his timing was wrong.

Electricity

"I want to buy your electricity." Trygve pumped the man's hand. "I'm Chris Lee. I recently bought land by the train depot out in the three corners area."

"Here at Hudson Light and Power we are always happy to expand. What is your address?"

"Well, that's the problem. I live off of Sawyer's Road, right over the town line in Bolton. But I want electricity from Hudson. I don't want to wait for Bolton or the Worcester power company."

"Well, let's see." The man motioned him back behind the counter to a large table where he rolled out a well-marked working map. The two men poured over the details of property lines and boundaries.

"We can't place a street pole past the town line. However, if you could get the owner of this property, your neighbor on the Hudson side, to agree to a pole on their property here… Well, then we could extend power to your residence Mr. Lee. But this address, your neighbors here, well, they are not currently power customers."

"I'll be back." And with many thanks, Chris

headed out to his new neighbor, Mrs. Larouche. Chris had just met his widowed neighbor who lived there with her adult son and worried unnecessarily that she would not be interested in the investment of electricity, to say nothing of an electric pole on their property. The Larouches, it turned out, had been talking about getting electricity for some time and were eager to help. They readily agreed.

Relieved, Trygve hopped in his car and headed up the street and home. "Valle, Valle, we are going to get electricity!" He planted an unusually enthusiastic kiss on her forehead.

"David, girls, come to eat. I have some exciting news."

"Are we going to get a 'radio'?" "We've been starving waiting for you."

The final platters were placed on the table, they held hands and recited grace.

"I went to the Light and Power company office after work. Made it there just before they closed and made my appeal for our case." He paused and looked up triumphantly, "The fish is good. Did you get it today?"

"Yes, cod, fresh from the peddler and I paid a pretty price. And now it is overdone. You were late."

There were a few moments of silence while everyone hungrily ate and chewed.

Valle broke the silence. "What do we need electricity for? We have nothing here that uses electricity. We are perfectly fine." And then with an added emphasis. "I am content. What more could we possibly need with electricity?" Valle shook her head and continued, "Won't you just be bringing in problems? Is it dangerous to bring this thing in our house? Can it cause a fire?"

Trygve sighed. "It's been around now for a while. All the new houses are being built with the wiring right in the construction. You seemed to enjoy electricity when we lived in Hudson. It's safe."

Little Dorothy piped up, "Uncle Hans and Aunt Margit have electric lights. Their house is beautiful." Harriet gave her sister a side eye and a quiet 'shhh...'"

"Valle, we don't have anything here that uses electricity because we do not get electricity. But we could have light, electric lamps." and he added softly, "And a radio."

"A radio," Valle looked up at her husband. "And what does that bring into the house? What kind of stories or music? I am content with our Victrola. You are the head of the house. You are supposed to protect us from worldly things and ungodly ideas. Foolishness." Then she took a pause before she added, "Why would you allow something you have no control over into the house?"

"Well, you do have control," he insisted, "You can choose what you listen to. And you turn it on or off." He continued carefully, "What about a refrigerator? What did you think of the ones we looked at last week at the store in Hudson? Wouldn't it be easier to keep food? And no more ice melting or water all over the floor."

"They cost too much. And don't tell me we are

going to have any debt or any payment plans. I'll not have it. Buying something before you pay for it." She shook her head. "It is like stealing. And what about the poor iceman? What will he do for a living if we all have electricity?"

"Actually, the ice company is already moving on to sell lumber. But," Trygve realized arguing was not going to work, "I realize it is a big change." He served himself more fish and potatoes and contemplated his next move.

And then little Dorothy piped up again, "Aunt Margit has a new refrigerator too. It's beautiful."

Valle gave a sigh. Later alone with Trygve, Valle acknowledged electricity was here to stay and would be part of their lives. Trygve was able to stop by the Hudson Light and Power office later that week and make plans for them to come out and survey the land.

Major

The children began attending school in Bolton. Every morning the school 'barge' would stop at the base of the hill by their home to pick up all the South Bolton. The barge was more like a long, roofed, open air flatbed truck with benches on either side. The children sat on benches on either side of the long cart facing each other. In the winter, the barge became an open horse drawn sleigh and the children huddled in deep straw to keep them warm. Dorothy went to the Emerson School and David and Harriet attended the Bolton Junior High School next to the town hall and First Congregational Church. The school barge picked them up every morning and brought them home in the afternoon. Valle was home alone all day.

Now that Valle had been in the neighborhood awhile and the house was in livable shape, she did begin to warm, slightly, to the idea of getting a dog. Trygve asked around and heard of a family eager to give up a young German Shepard they could not handle and Trygve jumped at the chance to own a family dog and a guard dog. Major was a typical sleek -bodied German Shepherd, with a black face and black and brown markings, his eyes bright, tongue wagging and eager.

Trygve and David came home with the dog and opened the car doors, and the dog took off in a furious blur to race around the car and family, circling at breakneck speed with the rope leash trailing behind. Trygve stomped around trying to step on the leash finally caught the leash, the dog jumped up on him and took off to run circles around Trygve, nearly toppling and tripping him up. The dog took to jumping up on him, barking, tongue lolling, and jumping up on Dorothy, nearly knocking her over, jumping up at David,

All the while Valle stood to the side, wiping her hands on her apron and watching with bemused seriousness. Then the dog jumped up towards Valle, studied her face and stopped in mid-air. The dog sat and faced Valle, her arms now akimbo, his nostrils flaring. The dog looked up at Valle, his head side to side, quizzically focused on her.

"Well, he already knows where his food is going to come from. How old is he?"

"He is 5 months old, Valle. He is trained, Valle, he's house trained. There should be no problems with that." Valle gave her husband a hard look, as if to say that better be true. Trygve continued his pitch to make the dog acceptable, "Valle, he's a real police dog. The family in town that had him couldn't handle him. They hated to give him up. They did not know how to train him. He needed more room. But he's a real police dog. His name is Major, he'll be a good dog."

"He better be. He has big paws. I suppose he

will still grow some. Well, we'd better feed him right away so he knows this is his new home. I'll get him something to eat." Father and son gave each other relieved looks.

The Fair and the Church

The Lee family climbed into the car one fine Saturday morning in September to head to the town fair. The Bolton Fair was the community event of the year. With sun hats and comfortable clothes, the family set off to discover more about their new hometown.

The center of town was barely a center; one small store, a post office and a line of square, austere but stately colonial homes on either side of the main road. A steepled church presided on a hill overlooking the entrance to the fair. The annual event attracted people from the surrounding area so the usually quiet town was now bursting with the crowd. People streamed down the street, past the pond on the corner, and down toward the new school building and surrounding grounds.

Newly fenced areas held pens of noisy hogs, chickens, goats, and dairy cows, dotted with blue ribbons here and there. A small group of official looking men with clipboards conferred in the hog pen, judging the best and biggest hogs. There were exhibits from local merchants including fresh apple cider pressed from Bolton orchards. David met some children he knew from school and took off to buy some food and pop. Dorothy got a pony ride.

They headed into the school and indoor exhibits and an official looking man standing by his sales exhibit spotted Trygve, "Chris, Chris Lee, how are you doing? How is my best customer enjoying the fair?" And now Trygve, known as Chris to non -Norwegians, was vigorously shaking hands with the man under the "Lamson Lumber, Hudson" sign and exhibit.

"I'm surprised to see you here indoors."

"Well, Chris, we wanted to show off the tools we are now featuring. Look at this hammer. It's called a claw hammer and let me show you how very useful it is." He pounded a couple of nails into a board set up for this purpose. A small group crowded around. "This hammer not only has the weight and strength needed but can also be used to easily pull OUT an unwanted nail." Mr. Lamson proceeded to demonstrate and used the claw to slip under the nail and with a twist of the hand, pulled the nail out.

"Look at that. Here." The demonstrator handed the hammer to Chris to feel the weight in his hand. The featured hammer was passed around the crowd as they contemplated this new invention.

"But not only that! Look, what we will also soon be carrying in the store: an electric drill." Oohs and aahs from the crowd as Mr. Lamson showed a rather bulky looking drill that, if plugged into an electric outlet, could drill a hole through wood ''like a warm knife through butter''.

By now Valle and the girls were edging away

and looking at exhibits of canned foods, jellies, breads and pies, some already garnished with blue or red ribbons.

Harriet pointed out the selection of cakes, "Ma, you should submit your cake. And if you make any jams next year. I bet yours are just as good." Then Harriet walked over to an official looking woman with a clipboard. "Excuse me Ma'am, these cakes just look delicious. How do you go about submitting your entry into the competition?"

"I am glad you are enjoying our display. I am afraid you would have to be a Bolton resident to enter any of the competitions."

"Oh, but we are. We just moved here, didn't we Ma." Harriet turned to her mother.

"Yes, how do you do? I am Valle Lee, and these are my daughters Harriet and Dorothy. We just moved to Bolton. We live off Sawyer Road, right near the train depot at the Hudson and Berlin lines."

"Oh, oh, yes, there."

"We live right across the street from Hog Swamp." Dorothy added with enthusiasm.

"Well. Yes, welcome to Bolton. I am Mrs. Sawyer, Leah Sawyer. There are a lot of us Sawyers in Bolton. So glad that you are enjoying our fair. And you can easily submit an entry next year. We look forward to it. Well. I must go now but it's so nice to meet you."

Exhausted by the afternoon, the family went home content with what they had learned their new hometown. Trygve had new tools to think about and had met Mr. Baginski who owned the pig farm near them in South Bolton. Hog Swamp was named after all his pigs who were so often lost in that swamp. Trygve discussed renting some pigs to clear out tree stumps from the field to enlarge his garden. Valle was quite pleased with herself that she had three successful English conversations; the Mrs. Sawyer, and the mother of one of David's friends, and another official judging the goats. Valle and Trygve wanted to buy a goat soon, so they gathered some contacts from the goat judges.

Feeling flush with self-confidence, Valle and Trygve decided to attend church in Bolton the next day. While living in Halden, Norway, or Hudson, the family had attended the neighborhood Methodist churches. The nearest Scandinavian Evangelical church was their beloved church in Concord but was a 15mile drive. Today they would check out the First Congregational Church in the center of Bolton.

The white colonial church sat on a pleasant site on Powder Hill overlooking the main route through town. The historic hill was once used for the secret storage of gunpowder for the Sons of Liberty in Revolutionary War times. The steepled church had simple small paned windows and white wooden pews.

Sunday morning the Lee family joined their Bolton neighbors and sat together in the colonial church. A small choir sang a lovely anthem and led the congregation in the doxology. The minister had a deep baritone voice and spoke about justice and peace in the world. The piano was slightly off key and the hymn singing tepid. As they left the service

Valle noticed her friend from the fair across the room and the two gave each other a little wave.

Once in the car, Harriet piped up, "Are we going to go to church here?"

"Why, what did you think of the service?" Trygve asked her.

"Well, it was okay. The pianist wasn't very good. The piano needs tuning. So, it wasn't all her fault."

She added, "I think others in my class go to Sunday School there."

David added, "Yeah, kids from my class go there."

Later after dinner when they were alone Valle made her feelings known to Trygve, "I did not understand that sermon. What was he even saying? His ideas were not focused on scripture."

"Yes, we are not going to get good Bible teaching at a church so watered down in their ideas about the Bible. These are the types who believe the Bible teaches good things, rather than believing it teaches the truth. I do not know. The children would benefit from being with their friends, but I'd like to get something out of the sermon."

"The children need good teaching, too. I think we must drive to Concord every Sunday. And I would miss our friends there if we started coming here."

"You are right. We'll drive there. The worship and music is better, too."

The Lee forged ahead to continue their commitment to the Scandinavian Evangelical church there.

The Fight

Trgve's plan to enlarge the family garden meant work for everyone.

First Trygve had, with a saw and ax, chopped down the trees scattered over the flat area designated for a garden. After the trees were moved off the land, Mr. Baginski arrived with his pigs and fencing. The pig farmer and Trygve securely fenced in the area to keep any more hogs from escaping and swimming around Hog Swamp. The pigs were let alone and allowed to do their best and root out those stumps. The three large hogs entertained the neighborhood children and enjoyed being well fed for their work as they grunted and dug up the land, clearing out the tree stumps and roots. Their work accomplished; the hogs went back home to continue to be fattened up by Mr. Baginski.

On this warm October Saturday morning, Trygve's plan meant the Lee children were out in full force picking rocks out of this uprooted section of land. With rakes and shovels, David and Trygve turned over soil the hogs had done their good work to and the girls followed behind and filled the wheelbarrow with rocks. Of course, Dorothy spent most of the time playing in the dirt and dawdling all she could and Harriet, who avoided any yard work arguing that she needed to practice the piano or help her mother in the house, never lasted long. But Saturday morning chores were Saturday morning chores and taken seriously no matter how boring. So while David and Trygve sweated and labored, the grumbling sisters joined in gleaning rocks and throwing them into a wheelbarrow.

Today Trygve was anxious to clear a section of the garden before winter weather set in and he gently but firmly encouraged the children in their labor. After overturning all the soil and clearing the rocks, he was planning to move a hen house over this area for the winter, ensuring an enlarged fertilized plot for the family garden ready for spring planting. Then he would move the hen house to fertilize a new spot. The children dawdled and complained; but Trygve persevered, envisioning and tasting future strawberries and fresh asparagus.

The plaintive chords from Clara's zither filled the air. The Leahy family was in a less productive mood than the Lees and had gathered for refreshments on the porch.

"Pa, Clara is singing again," David said.

"I know, I can hear her." I can hear them all is what Trygve was thinking.

The entire Fahey family was there at the house next door enjoying a Saturday celebration filled with moonshine, apparently celebrating the visit of Milly and James, Mary's parents. The drunken party had spilled out on their small porch on this warm fall day. Jim's grandchildren played in the grass, just yards from the laboring Lee family. Clara's soulful voice spilled out over the neighborhood. Her daughter loudly joined her, while her husband James raised his mason jar toasting each chorus.

At the chorus, with great moonshine infused gusto, they crooned together,

> *But your soul, so pure and sweet,*
> *Makes my____happiness complete*
> *Makes me falter at your feet, Sweet Marie.*

Grandpa Leahy sat silently drinking his homemade moonshine in his rocking chair in the corner. Gladys peeked out the window from inside.

Down the street, Mr. Wilson was out front at his house, working on his car and talking to an insurance agent out on his rounds. Both observed the drunken party with some amusement.

Grandpa Jim Fahey had continued through the years to enjoy his homemade brew without incident. Neighbors had mostly minded their own business. Every child in the neighborhood knew exactly where Grandpa's still was located, right up against the house and camouflaged with foliage. In fact the entertainment for the neighborhood children was to sneak through the woods and lie at the top of a ledge in the rear of the house to get a good view and watch Grandpa working at his still. No one snitched. Or no one admitted that they snitched.

On the many other occasions when it was obvious their neighbors were enjoying their illegal brew, Trygve and Valle Lee had continued in their resolve to mind their own business.

But now Saturday morning was suddenly filled with the sound of shattering glass. James threw a mason jar in anger. The shattering glass sounded like an explosion. The zither was silent. The singing ended. Valle bolted out of the house at the sound. James yelled something at his wife. Milly stood, screaming up in his face. All eyes were on the pair.

"Don't you ever talk to me like that," James looked down at his wife and slapped her hard across the face. There was sudden silence on the porch. Milly cowered in her mother's arms.

Like a clanging gong or a sudden bellow, Trygve's deep voice broke the silence,

"That's it. That's enough." echoed through the trees. And Trygve Christian Lee threw down his shovel and strode across to their porch like a general marching off to war, leaping up the stairs, he grabbed a startled James Fahey by the shirt and threw him down the steps. James, stunned and drunk, rolled down the couple of stairs like a rubber ball. As the drunk man struggled to get his feet. Trygve glowered over him and bellowed again, "Get up."

Then Trygve leaned down and grabbed him by the shirt collar, pulling the much taller man to his feet, slamming him against the house.

Trygve snarled in his face, "You want to hit someone? Hit someone who can hit back." Trygve pushed back and bobbed in front of the confused man, with his bare fists pummeling the air. James stood and shook off his confusion, stepped aside and then took his stance. James put up his dukes, too; his arms and fists waving through the air haphazardly. The two men danced a bit, sizing up their opponent, circling. Then James threw a tentative first swing. Trygve ducked and landed a quick left jab. Now both men were awake.

James Fahey, tall and lanky, had the longer reach. Trygve was shorter but powerful and had the advantage of being sober. Fists flew. James leaned in to swing and Trygve got a quick upper clip. Then Trygve took a punch full to the nose and his full fury unleashed. Powerful quick jab after jab followed with each man landing a shower of blows. The pummeling slowed. James and Trygve each danced back on his feet. Then Trygve moved in with one powerful swing landing full to the side of James's face and James went down, lying in a wretched heap on the dusty road. He moaned.

"Get up," Trygve's booming command echoed through the neighborhood. The families and neighbors stood silently, aghast and stunned at this display of violence. No one had moved since the spectacle began.

"I said, 'Get up.'" The command seemed to hang in the air. James struggled to his knees, his hand over his mouth, and he swayed slowly to his feet.

Trygve stood firmly before him, bloodied, and battered but not blinking. Fist in the air punctuating every syllable of his threat, he declared, "If I ever see you hit a woman again, you won't get up."

There were audible gasps from the audience. The scene seemed to morph into a silent slowmotion film. James continued to sway. He removed his hand from his mouth and turned and looked squarely at his opponent as blood dribbled down his chin. He made a groan like a sick cow and spit blood. The blood spattered onto the ground with one tooth gleaming white in the crimson stream and puddle.

Trygve's battered face went white. Now Trygve began to sway.

Slowly and cautiously, James walked backwards toward the house.

David and Valle had raced to Trygve's side, each grabbing him up under his arms on either side. Practically dragging him, and hoping that after whipping his opponent into submission, he would not faint on them, the two managed to drag Trygve around to the back of the house. Trygve was able to pull himself up the back steps and lean over the porch railing as he retched.

Out front of the house, on the dirt road, all had scattered. The soulful music and chords of the zither, the chatter of neighbors and quiet sounds of an ordinary day, had gone silent. For anyone listening beyond the birds and buzz of nature, all was silent except the hacking cough of heaving and retching and an occasional low moan coming from the Lees'.

Tryge shook his head as he hung over the railing. "Valle, Valle, Valle," he said softly as he shook his head. "Valle, I hit a man."

"Yes, you certainly did."

"Pa, you got him good. You really know how to land a punch." At that reminder, Trygve heaved again.

"Help me get him inside. See if we can get him

on the couch." Harriet had towels out on the couch already and a bucket nearby. Dorothy in the living room, watched from afar. Trygve finally lay quietly on the couch.

Valley handed David some money from the pitcher above the stove. "Here, go to Mrs. McCarthy's and see if you can buy some ice. Tell her it is an emergency. No, you do not have to tell her the details. No one needs to know. See if she has any Parker Rolls available, even some day-olds. When your father is feeling better, he might be able to eat something soft."

Valle gently washed her husband's face. "You're going to be a little black and blue my dear."

"I can't believe I hit him," Trygve moaned.

"You did a good thing. You did good. How are your teeth?" Valle asked her husband, examining his face and mouth.

"Nothing loose." Trygve answered. "What did I do? Oh Valle. What does God think of me? God forgive me, I hurt a man. And what will people think? "

Valle gently wiped his brow. "God would have more to forgive if you had done nothing. Don't worry about God for this. No one else has to know. Did you hurt your hands? Let me see your hands. I think we'll have fewer drunken parties around here."

Soon David came bounding in with his hands full. "Here's the money. Mrs. McCarthy wouldn't take any money. Here's the ice. She gave us some fresh Parker rolls and an apple pie."

"Apple pie?" his parents chorused.

"Yeah." Out of breath from excitement David continued, "She said 'good job; and all that. She was happy to give us the ice. Said you deserved it. She already knew about it and all. The fight that is."

Trygve groaned. "Ugh, everyone will know. Oh, what will people think?"

"Well," Valle was thoughtful, "I guess it is better we don't keep secrets anyway."

The Search

Monday was baking day. Bread was already in the oven filling the house with its yeasty aroma; the large yellow crockery bowl was filling up with the bulging second batch. Packing four lunches every morning required a steady production of loaves of bread. The family now enjoyed some variety for lunch with bologna or cheese added to the menu of the less desirable sliced boiled potato sandwich.

Major followed Valle's every move with particular intensity on baking day, staying close to her feet as she completed her chores. The dog never rested; his nose down, tongue out, he followed his beloved owner in and out the house, as she fed the chickens or hung the clothes to dry. He stood silently at her side as she mixed or measured or kneaded, patiently waiting for the morsel of food that rarely came. Occasionally the dog would be stuck on the wrong side of the screen door, forgotten and abandoned, he would stand or sit patiently; his ears pricked and head alert, waiting for Valle to return, so he could continue his overt mission.

"Oh, would you get out of my way, shoo,"

Valle opened the oven doors to retrieve the browned loaves and set them to cool. Then like a shot, Major lunged to the front door, barking, running to the windows, to the side door, barking and jumping to look out the windows.

"Stop it. Quiet." Valle commanded and then she also heard the unusual sound of a motor car driving up the street. The black sedan stopped in the street between the Lees' and the Leahys' front steps.

Valle stepped out on the porch, just managing to grab Major's collar as he ran out at her side. Two men in dark suits stepped out on either side of the car. They stood there staring at the dog as they each stood behind the open car doors. The driver removed his hat, "Good afternoon, I am Officer Murphy, and I am here with Mr. Brown. We are US Marshals, well, we are just checking out a complaint. Well, ma'am, ma'am, that is a mighty fine-looking dog you have there. Uh, would you mind hanging on to, umm, controlling that dog so we could ask you a few questions?"

"Yes, he is very obedient," Valle dragged Major into the house, leaning over and giving Major a good scratch behind the ears, and a quiet, "Good boy." Valle stood up and gave a firm "Stay," with a firm palm up hand gesture. She let go of his collar and turned her attention to the two agents still standing behind the shelter of the car doors. Behind Valle the screen door noisily slammed, then bounced open, to flap again and again, slower and slower, swinging loosely, until it finally stopped. Major stood, glaring behind the unsecured screen door.

Valle stood at the top of the porch stairs and waited.

The men did not move from their sheltered positions but finally continued, "We had a complaint about the neighbors here concerning the possible production and distribution of liquor, or moonshine. So, we wanted to take a walk around here."

"We could show our credentials," He flipped open a black wallet.

"That is not necessary," Valle answered.

"Do you have any idea of where this stuff is made? Or where the still is located?" The other agent asked Valle.

"No," she shook her head.

"Could I ask you how long you have lived here?" He continued.

"Two years."

The driver added, "If you could restrain your dog in some way, Ma'am, we would appreciate it. We would like to walk around your neighbor's house and search through the woods around here. And thank you for your cooperation."

"Of course. I can tie him up," and she picked up a rope on the porch and proceeded to leash Major. The men slowly backed up, shut the car doors and headed for Leahy's house.

Valle could see that the shades were drawn, and Gladys was not visible at her usual place by the window. The men walked into the woods around the back of the house and then headed into the woods.

Major gave another excited bark as the school barge came to a squeaky stop and parked at the bottom of the hill, spilling out the neighborhood students.

David was first, running up to his mother, "Whose car is this?"

"Here, you take care of the dog. Police of some sort are looking for the still. They do not want Major to eat them. Come in."

David laughed, "Major might lick them to death. Where are these guys going?"

"Well, no," his mother responded, "not if Major was protecting one of us from a stranger. They may very well have reason to fear Major protecting us. The agents walked around Leahy's house and back into the woods behind the houses here."

David shook his head laughing. "These guys are never going to find..."

"No," his mother interrupted him. "Say nothing. I do not want to know a thing. Your father and I do not want to be involved. I am not going to lie or to defend their behavior. Let the sheriff or police do what they need to do. But there is no reason for us to be involved or watching and reporting on our neighbors. We are to love our neighbors and show neighborly love by example." Valle sighed and added, "However, nothing good comes from drink."

The children each had one thick slice of warm bread, fresh from the oven with butter. Harriet had work to do and piano practice. David and Dorothy headed out to explore and join the other neighboring kids as they enjoyed watching these two men stumble through the brush and bushes looking for the elusive still hiding in plain sight.

Major enjoyed an extra helping of stew meat that evening for dinner.

Nanny the Goat and Unwelcome Visitors

Valle and Trygve brought Dorothy with them when they went to a nearby farm. They purchased Nanny, a young milking goat. The children would be back in school soon and Valle would have one more animal to keep her company. "Nanny" had a black face and brown, gray and black markings. Dorothy was wedged in the back seat, holding onto the goat's halter and laughing as the goat nuzzled her and nibbled on her hair ribbon.

"She's going to eat my ribbon. No, now she's after my collar!" Dorothy giggled as the goat tickled her and nuzzled her. "Oh, she is so sweet. I love this goat. I love you, Nanny."

"Good," said Trygve. "You can help your mother take care of her. Although goats aren't too hard to care for, she'll still need tending."

"I'm looking forward to the milk. I can teach you how to milk her," Valle added.

"Ma, do you think Major will get along with her?"

"Yes, animals that live together usually end up accepting each other. Major may want to herd her and guard her little. They will adjust," Valle explained.

The little 'barn' was already for Nanny when they got home. She had an area fenced for her and a comfortable home in the barn.

Nanny received a lot of attention from David and his friends. Everyone wanted to pet her, and she was very friendly. She ate every treat, carrot, or apple they gave her, and bounded around the barn like an acrobat. Major watched with interest and only barked at the children.

Dinner time came and everyone went home or into the house. The Lee family had just said grace. Harriet stood up to bring the butter to the table and screamed when she looked out the kitchen window.

"That goat is eating my blouse! My favorite Blouse!" There was Nanny, happily munching on the clothes on the clothesline, chewing away on the lace fringes of a white blouse.

Valle and Harriet ran out first and grabbed their new pet by the collar and led her back to her indoor home.

"We made you this nice home and corral, how did you get out?" Valle exclaimed at the goat.

"Ma, I was planning on wearing that blouse. It's ruined," Harriet cried.

"We need to get you some new clothes anyway for school. I can't believe it. We can order something from the Sears catalog or go shopping in Hudson this weekend."

Nanny did not seem to appreciate her lovely new home and managed to find a way to jump the fence and sample the garden or roam the neighborhood, sampling the neighbor's flowers or bushes. Mrs. Boucher was startled one morning to find Nanny at her front door expecting a handout. Trygve added more boards and filled in any possible points in the fence where Nanny could escape.

On Saturday the Lee family headed to downtown Hudson. David needed new shoes. He would continue at Bolton junior high school. The seventh, eighth, and ninth grades met there in the three-room schoolhouse. Two teachers taught the three grades, rotating through the classes one after another, while the unattended class worked on their assignments.

Dorothy attended the elementary school across the street from the junior high school and she enjoyed school. Dorothy loved the music and art classes best. Every Friday they would have a music appreciation class. The students listened to a radio program and learned about different composers each week.

But Harriet would move on and attend Hudson High School. Each day she would catch the post office's mail truck and she and two other Bolton students would catch this ride into Hudson center and go to high school there in the morning. After school the mail truck going in the opposite direction back to Bolton would give them transportation. But now they needed clothes.

David got his new shoes. Harriet got two new blouses. Valle found some pillows for her and Trygve. Dorothy was happy with a new dress.

When they got home from their shopping,

Nanny was not to be found.

"Where is that goat?" Valle exclaimed.

"Is this goat worth all the trouble?" Harriet asked as they made quick plans to spread out. David planned to go down the street one way, Trygve headed for the car to drive around the neighborhood, and the girls went in different directions. But before they got very far, Mrs. Boucher came walking into view with the escapee firmly in her grip.

"You'd better keep a leash on this goat. She gets lonely when you leave her so she is always going to wander if she can," Mrs. Boucher was smiling but also shaking her head a bit.

"Why do we have this goat?" Harriet asked. "This animal is so much work. And I hate goat's milk," she added.

"I love her. I love Nanny. You are just mean," Dorothy defended her beloved pet.

"I don't see you milking her," Harriet responded. "Have you tried drinking her milk? Give me good ole dairy milk from a cow."

"We drank goat's milk all the time growing up. I don't know what you are talking about Harriet," Valle responded. "Let's give this poor goat a chance."

The next few days Nanny stayed in her fenced area or barn. She came when called or maybe when she thought someone had a treat for her.

The first days of school started. The New England weather gave one last hot breath of summer and everyone was sweltering. Between the tension of a new school year and the heat, no one slept well. Valle had to go upstairs and make sure the children were up. David could not find his book. Harriet was upset about her hair. Dorothy could not find her socks. Trygve and Valle particularly were uncomfortable. It was the second day of the new school year. Valle had the bologna sandwiches made. Apples for everyone. Four lunch boxes filled. And Trygve came downstairs in a panic.

"Valle, look" Trygve exclaimed. "I haven't been able to sleep because I itch so. Look at my legs," he pulled up his pants and showed her little red marks.

"Oh, I have them on my arm...Oh, oh no!"

They both looked at each other. "Bedbugs. The new pillows."

"I have to leave for work, but I'll drag the mattress outside right now." And he did. He took pillows, sheets, and a blanket all outside and left them in a heap. Then he and Valle dragged the mattress down and out the door. "Valle, I'll burn the mattress when I get home. Don't touch it."

"Don't touch anything," Trygve growled a bit at the children. "We have bed bugs from those new pillows. Don't touch that mattress! Just get your stuff and catch your rides. It'll be okay."

"Don't worry, I won't touch anything," Harriet assured her parents with an eye roll. The children all ate their oatmeal and then grabbed their lunches and eagerly left for their rides.

Valle stood in the suddenly empty house and looked around. She sat for a minute drinking her coffee, deciding what task to do first. Even as she wiped her brow, she knew heat would kill bed bugs. And she wanted the bed bugs dead. She had to take care of the chickens and Nanny and feed the dog. Then the bed bugs needed to be eradicated.

She marshaled her plan. In the shed was the old oil stove she used for canning. She filled a large pot with water and started boiling the sheets. She could not fit them all in at one time so it would be a long process. Once that was started, she went upstairs and considered the coil springs of the bed. She cleared the chairs from the room and gathered her supplies. She would need a bucket or two of water in case there was a fire. She gathered all the candles and matches she could find. She thought it would be easier if she could elevate the bed frame but needed something that would not easily burn or slip. She raised the bed with bricks and began the task at hand.

The cloth mattress padding and the pillows were outside in a heap to be burnt. But the coil springs that were normally under the padding were the perfect hiding place for the tiny bed bugs. The only way to be sure they were rid of the nuisance was to heat each coil hot enough to kill any bug that might be hiding in the coils. And so Valle lay on the floor under the coils and with a lit candle, heated each and every coil, working methodically from coil to coil, row to row. She marked each row.

Valle had to take breaks. The sweat dripped down her face. Her arms ached. She sweated as she finished boiling all the linens and hanging them out to dry. Bed bugs or not, her family would need to eat dinner. Instead of the meal she was planning, to save time she took all the ingredients, kielbasa sausage, potatoes, carrots, and cabbage and threw them on a large casserole and into the oven. She opened all the windows.

Dorothy and David came home and saw their mother finishing heating up the last of the coils. "Don't come in here and stay away from the mattress outside. I am almost finished here. I just have to wash the floor when these coils cool," Valle explained to her children.

"I'm going to give Nanny her treats," Dorothy headed to the basement to get some carrots out of the barrel of sand in the root cellar.

Harriet yelled from the front door, "Ma, that goat's made a mess of the sheets on the clothesline. And she is eating the mattress out in the yard. And the pillows!"

"Well, go get her and put her back in the barn, "Valle yelled from upstairs.

Harriet threw her book bag on the floor and off she went, "Dorothy, are you supposed to be taking care of this goat? Where are you?"

David appeared to help round up the illusive animal. First, they had to catch Nanny. She was snacking on one of the contaminated pillows, dragging the pillow into the garden.

"Don't touch the pillow," David warned.

"Well, how are you supposed to wrangle her up without doing that?" Harriet complained.

"Dorothy, get her one of the treats and lead her back into the barn. We don't want to touch that bed bug pillow," Valle warned.

Dorothy rummaged through a few rows of the

last of the garden and emerged with a couple of small tomatoes to lead Nanny back to her home.

Valle finished cleaning the previously defiled room and got dinner on the table. They were able to sit down for their hot meal. Suddenly Harriet slammed down her glass of milk. "Ma, is this goat milk? Did you put goat's milk in the regular milk container? Are you trying to trick us?"

"I am not trying to trick you. But goat's milk is good to drink. I thought if it was nice and cold you would all like it."

Trygve frowned, "You eat what is put on the table. And no complaining." Then he paused and added, softening his tone, "Your mother has had a busy day in this heat cleaning and ridding the house of these bed bugs. I still have to go out and burn what is left of the mattress that the goat has not already eaten or spread around the yard."

Dorothy piped up bravely, "It's not all Nanny's fault. Everyone says that Nanny would be much happier with another goat. She is lonely. Goats don't like to live alone. Can we get another goat to keep her company? I'll take care of them."

There was a chorus of "No."

Trygve added, "No more goats." His voice got softer. They could barely hear him, "And I too think we can stick to cow's milk from the store."

The Argument

David was recuperating from Quincy's throat. For weeks David had lain in bed taking over his distraught parents' room, the windows open to let in the cold of winter so he could breathe fresh clean air. The doctor had visited, watching over his young patient bundled in quilts, the snow gathering on the windowsill as they spoke with hushed voices and white breaths. Now the fever had broken, the danger had passed, and everyone in the Lee household walked a little lighter and spoke more brightly, and the house was warmer.

Trygve drove by himself to his brother-in-law's to make a payment on the mortgage. He had left that morning with a spring in his step after David's recovery and a conversation with his wife about how quickly they were paying off their mortgage debt.

Although the family had not attended church that Lord's day, Valle and the girls had enjoyed making David's favorite Sunday-coming-home - from-church dinner of pot roast and potatoes and vegetables simmering in the oven all morning and filling the house with a warm aroma on a cold day.

The cream pudding that would soon be slathered with melted butter and cinnamon, sat ready on the counter. The table was set; the food prepared.

Finally, Trygve returned from his lengthy errand. The hungry family gathered; David, a little pale but smiling, came down the stairs, Dorothy joined her sister gathering the serving utensils and platters, and Valle greeted her husband at the door.

"How many more months to pay this off?" she asked and gave him a peck on the cheek.

"Well, it could be sooner than we planned my dear."

"Oh, how is that?"

"Well," and Trygve became quiet and suddenly sober as he looked at his wife's face. "Well," he continued.

"Come into the kitchen. I have to get the meat out of the oven."

Trygve hung his coat on the coat rack, removed a folded piece of paper, and followed his wife into the kitchen and stood by the door, watching Valle take the large covered roasting pan out of the oven.

"Well, why are we going to pay this debt off quicker?" Valle asked with interest.

He cleared his throat. "Your brother is a very smart man, Valle. Working at a bank and all…"

Valle turned, her arms akimbo, and faced her husband. "I know my brother works at a bank. What has that got to do with us?"

There was momentary silence as they stared at each other. Then she asked,

"What did you do, Trygve Christian Lee? What do you have in your hand?"

Trygve took a deep breath, "Valle, your brother explained to me how we could pay off our debt to him much faster, well, we could use our money to make money." Valle was stone still and staring into his face.

Trygve shuffled a bit and continued, "We give him our mortgage payment every month to pay him back, and he turns around and buys stocks and makes double, sometimes, on the very money that WE have given him in payment. Hans, your brother, is trying to be helpful to us. Valle, so we can pay off our mortgage…" He got quieter, "sooner."

~

"So we pay off the mortgage sooner by not making our regular payment? My brother is indeed a smart man if he can pull that off. But you are right, husband. 'We' is right. You and I, husband and wife, we make a payment on OUR debt. And I thought we both agreed that we would not gamble with OUR money? And how, in God's name, did you come to agree that not putting money toward our mortgage, would pay it off sooner? How did my brother concoct such a fancy trick?"

Harriet, Dorothy, and David sat awkwardly in the next room at the table, not moving.

"It is not gambling to invest our money in the future of a company. Valle, Hans, your brother …"

"Hans, my brother? I don't care if you talked to Moses or Saint Peter himself; you and I had an agreement. We agreed to pay this mortgage off. We agreed we would not, WOULD NOT, use our money to buy these so called stocks, we would not be tempted to throw our money away, to use debt to make money. We would not be tempted by greed to gamble our money, hoping to make a quick buck, tomorrow, when we could pay off our real debt today. 'Hans my brother' Who is Hans? He's no saint and no authority for our family. 'Hans your brother'. Valle shook her head and sighed. "Ha. I will not live under a roof where God is mocked. This is gambling."

Trygve sighed and spoke softly, "Valle, an investment in stocks for a company is not the same as gambling. We have purchased part of the future earnings of a company, that's all. Look here," Trygve turned and opened up the stock certificate he now owned and laid it out on the kitchen table between them as they stood over the table and examined the certificate.

"It is a certificate. It is a formal document, Valle...Look 'American Telegraph and Telephone Company, the future...Valle..."

"Oh, it's a certificate. Of course. A certificate. Silly me. So it is okay to gamble and go further into debt for a certificate. You can dishonor God for an important CERTIFICATE.' Valle stared at her husband and the word seemed to hang in the air between them.

Trygve leaned over the kitchen table, fists clenched on the table and hung his head. His wife continued.

"If it is a debt today for money in the future then it is a form of gambling. Who can know the future? Suddenly you can see through time? This is gambling with our money. 'Thou shalt not covet' Right? We've talked about this before Trygve. How many times? "

By now the children had disappeared from the dining room table. David was reading the comics in a corner, with Major laying at his feet; the dog stared with a worried look, watching his owners in the kitchen. Harriet was curled in a chair leafing through her new music sheets and Dorothy had slipped upstairs and out of the way.

"'Thou shalt not covet.' Valle don't throw Bible verses at me. Valle, I think we both know that buying stocks is NOT actually gambling." Trygve added with determination.

"You don't want me to throw Bible verses at you? How about facts? You and I had decided to pay off our mortgage and be debt free. We had agreed to make that our goal. You and I, husband and wife, had decided to never borrow money to try to make money in the stock market. We have discussed this and come to this agreement that somehow you think one conversation with my brother can change. Because of course he works in a bank, and he is my big shot brother so I should agree? Is that it?"

"Valle, my dear," Trygve sat at the table, trying a more gentle approach. "I am sorry you are upset about this. I am only trying; your brother was only trying to help us. Many people, including your brother, are making money, benefitting their families, Valle. After all, he was willing to forgo a payment with no penalty or increase in the interest rate, so that we could have this opportunity." Trygve looked up hopefully into his wife's face.

"You know as well as I do, what the Bible

teaches about debt. FLEE debt. We were fleeing our debt and paying off this loan. Honoring God's word is more important than more money. More important for our future, our provision. Which, I might add, you and I had always agreed was from Him. He provides for us so why do we need to stoop to something that even smells of gambling or coveting? Do you need to read it again? Here. You don't want me to throw Bible verses at you?" Valley grabbed the Bible from a shelf, "Here is the whole thing." And she slammed the Bible down right in front of him with a thud as he ducked, the book barely missing his face.

"And this is what I think of your fancy certificate." Valle grabbed the document and took it to the stove where she lit a match and set it on fire. The fire lit at the bottom corner as she held it in the air, flames curling up the sides and burning the gold gilded edges, and ornately colored illustration. Valle dropped the mess on the stove top. A thin stream of smoke circled above the fire devouring the family's fifty dollars and filling the house with the harsh, acrid smell of burning paper.

The couple quietly watched the fires lick the last of the certificate.

Dorothy came running down the stairs wild eyed. "Pa, what is burning? Is the house on fire? I can smell something burning."

"Nothing, don't worry. I didn't mean to frighten you. We are just burning something that I should not have brought home. It is alright. Everything is alright. Don't worry. We will eat dinner in just a minute."

Trygve got up and walked over to his wife and put his arms loosely around her. They stood there for a minute in silence. Trygve spoke softly, "I am sorry. Forgive me. You are right. And may God provide for us as we honor Him. Even if I am a little halfhearted at times."

Trygve turned and spoke up, "I think everyone is hungry. Thank you for cooking this meal, Valle. David, Harriet, join us for dinner now." Major trotted in, tongue out and happy, he gave Trygve a nudge. "Yes, good boy, we'll feed you, too."

Harriet and David solemnly joined Dorothy and their parents at the table. They recited their grace.

In Jesus name we come to the table

To eat and to drink by the power of your

blessing

In honor of the Lord, so that we may

prosper.

There was a general sigh of relief as the family passed around the pot roast and potatoes and now enjoyed their meal.

Friday Night Radio

"Harriet, you'll have to stop practicing when the fight starts," Valle reminded her daughter. "

I know. I know. I just love this new song," And Harriet continued practicing the light melody.

"What is the name of the song?" Valle inquired.

"Oh it's '*When You're Smiling*', you've probably heard it before on the radio," Harriet replied and then resumed playing.

"Well, let's eat dessert before the fight. Dorothy, David, it is almost time for the fight. There is dessert if you want to finish it before the fight starts," Valle

Trygve put his paper down. The children gathered at the table to help themselves to rice pudding with blueberry compote and whipped cream.

"Anything of interest in the news today?" Valle asked.

"Well, Hoover signed in additional penalties for bootlegging. I don't know if it will do any good, but I guess at least he is trying something. Al

Capone will be dragged before the courts in Chicago next week. Maybe things will improve in the country."

"Pa, you don't sound convinced," David responded.

"We can give the new President some time. See what he can do. I liked that song you were practicing, Harriet."

"*'When You're Smiling'*, it's pretty popular," Harriet answered.

"Well, I am smiling," Valle said. Then she surveyed her family sitting around the dining room table and added, "I think we should be positive and be encouraged. And we will have the mortgage paid off in a few months. We are all healthy. God is good."

No one could contradict Valle or argue with that. So, they silently finished up their pudding.

Valle did have reason to feel confident. Harriet continues high school next year and is developing into a confident pianist. David plans on attending vocational high school in Worcester where he will get a good education and a trade. Dorothy is a happy child and loves school. The garden produces an overabundance of vegetables, the chickens are laying eggs, the children thrive. There is a new president in the White House. Even the Norwegian Evangelical church in Concord was flourishing and able to fully support two missionary families in China. Suddenly their life did not seem as rootless and fragile as Valle once feared.

Trygve was at the radio, finding the station.

"Let's see if Tommy can keep his

championship title." Trygve and Valle pulled up the living room chairs close to the radio. David sat on the floor. Major happily circled around in one spot in the middle of them until he settled down next to David, his tongue hanging out of his mouth, and flopped down in happy relief in the center of the circle of his family. The girls pulled up chairs. Their mouths and lips still slightly purple from all the blueberries, all to listen to the blow-by-blow description of the latest Friday night fight.

The music started. And the terse monologue from the announcer began:

"From Chicago Stadium, Chicago in a ten round box. Tommy Loughran is defending his World Light Heavy Weight Championship title against 'Toy Bulldog', Mickey Walker. A huge crowd here at Chicago Stadium to see Tony Loughran, the Stylist, defend his title. Walker, trying to win his third championship division against the favored Loughran."

The sound of the bell and Trygve and Valle, intent on the description of every blow, leaned in with their bodies tense. Trygve's fists tighten as he thought through every blow. The crowd cheered. The bell rang for each round. The Lees leaned in to listen and follow the announcer as the boxers went ten rounds. When the final round was over the announcer continued as the crowd cheered:

"Here's the decision. Tommy Lougran wins and keeps his title for another day."

Exhausted, the family cheered that their man had won the day.

"Ok, whew, that's over. I want to play this

song. Let's try to harmonize." Harriet explained.

Harriet sat at the piano with a sibling on either side reading the music sheet. "You've heard this before. It goes like this," she played the harmony for them. Then she went into the full piano introduction and the trio sang...

When you're smilin', when you're smilin'
The whole world smiles with you
When you're laughin', when you're laughin'
The sun comes shinin' through
But when you're cryin', you bring on the rain
So stop that cryin', be happy again
Keep on smilin', 'cause when you're smilin'
The whole world smiles with you

A Norwegian Christmas Eve
The Plan

The discussion began in summer. Valle received a package from her cousin Maud in Oslo containing the usual old Norwegian magazines Gladys sent her every so often. Valle loved to get the packages and read old gossip about the king and his family and pour over the recipes. Valle sat in the Adirondack chair under the pine trees, fanning herself in the heat and leafing through her pile.

"So what is new with Maud? She sent you a bunch of magazines. Anything of interest?" Trygve sat down next to his wife.

"Well, she sent a number of old Christmas issues this time. She must have decided to finally get rid of them all. So there are some interesting recipes. Too bad we can't get any nokkelost here or any good cheese." She turned to her husband. 'You know Christmas is the worst time of year for me. I can get so homesick. I especially miss the food, the cheese and chocolates, oh, everything."

"You still get homesick?" Trygve asked his wife.

"Yes, at Christmas, especially. And don't tell

me you don't. I can tell."

"Well, yeah I do." Trygve agreed.

She handed him some old Norwegian newspapers to read. They sat and read quietly. Then he piped up, "Valle, I could make lutefisk for Christmas Eve dinner if you want."

"Oh, lutefisk would be good. How long does it take to soak the fish? You could do it? I can ask around and see who has made it before in Norway. Maybe Margret or Ragnild, no, they left Norway when they were young…"

"Valle, you don't have to ask any of your women friends. Of course, I can make lutefisk. How hard can it be? Everyone makes it at home. Besides water there are two ingredients, lye and fish."

"Oh, how good that would be to look forward tolutefisk for Christmas Eve, maybe with creamed peas. And I can make lefse. It's been so long since I've had lefse! I don't know why my mother stopped making it."

Trygve added, "We'll have to also plan on going to the Concord church and have a real Norwegian Christmas Eve service as well."

"Oh, wouldn't it be nice to hear our children sing in Norsk."

And so the plan was hatched.

Trygve asked around at the Concord Evangelical Scandinavian Church not long after, asking his friends where they bought their dried cod for Christmas lutefisk. But the Gustavsens and Petersens shopped all the way in Boston. Worcester was closer and since there were enough Swedes living in Worcester for there to be a new Swedish bakery, Trygve hoped maybe someone at the bakery could tell him where he could buy dried cod. But it turned out he did not need to depend on Swedes after all. With all the Portuguese people living in Hudson, it turned out the local A & P carried dried cod regularly. So when December finally came around, the dried cod was purchased right at the local A&P from the fish section and Trygve prepared.

Trygve purchased rubber 'acid' gloves from Sears and Roebuck to protect his hands from the caustic marinade. He went to Larson Lumber to acquire the needed ingredients and a couple of wooden buckets.

Trygve hung the dried fish, which were stiff smelly balsa wood planks, from the ceiling in the basement. He would begin the soaking process about two weeks before Christmas Eve. In the meantime, the family had other Christmas plans.

Shopping

One Saturday morning the Lee family was up early and off on their annual Boston Christmas shopping day. Bundled up in coats and mittens and knitted hats. They headed out of the house and down to the train depot to catch the first morning train to Boston. Trygve loaded up on morning newspapers. The family members carefully folded and unfolded the papers, passing them around to each other, their heads buried in the papers. The train filled up with shoppers at each stop as they neared the city.

Dorothy read the funnies for a while until boredom overcame her and feeling free to say whatever she wanted in Norwegian in the crowded train, she spoke up,

"Are we going to have to eat that stinky fish hanging in the cellar for Christmas?"

"Why can't we have a turkey dinner or roast like everyone else?" Harriet added.

"What do you mean? When your father finishes soaking the fish and I cook it for dinner it will be delicious."

Valle looked up to see her three children

looking at her with blank, unimpressed stares. Dorothy's blonde braids sticking out of the knitted hat and her skinny arms hung out of the not quite long enough sleeves. Harriet looked perky in her blue and white knit hat with her brown curls and blue eyes. David too had skinny arms hanging out not long enough sleeves. Her slender children grew and grew.

"I ate this all the time in Norway, "she added. "We had lutefisk every Christmas Eve for dinner. It is so good with lots of butter. Besides, you all love fish."

"Not fish boiled in soap," moaned Dorothy.

"If it tastes so good, why don't other people eat it?" David asked.

"Norwegians eat it. And even the Swedes. And we don't boil it in soap. We soak the dried fish in lye."

"Ma, lye is soap. Will it be really mushy?" David asked.

Harriet retorted, "No, just slimy. I vaguely remember eating it at Besta's in Halden." She grimaced.

David continued, "Ma, most Americans don't buy ingredients for their Christmas dinner at a hardware store."

"I don't want slimy soapy Norwegian fish for Christmas, "Dorothy continued, almost crying, "Why can't we have good Boston fish?"

"Because we are Norwegians and Norwegians have lutefisk for Christmas Eve. And you will love it, I am sure," exasperated, Valle answered firmly.

.Trygve now slowly put down the

newspaper and looked at his family and the attentive passengers around them, waiting to overhear his family's next unintelligible retort. He spoke in English, looking sternly at each of them, "Children, why don't you tell your mother what you hope to get for Christmas." They were quiet for a few minutes.

Then Harriet interrupted the silence in Norwegian again, "You are going to make meatballs, too, though, right?"

"Yes. We will have plenty of meatballs."

The train pulled into Boston and the Lee family tumbled out with all the other shoppers and climbed on to the T to take the trolley to the shopping district on Washington Street.

The windows at the Jordan Marsh Department store were filled with treasures on display surrounded by the visual delights of the season, greenery and ribbons, lights and candles, and animated carolers whose mouths opened and shut as they sang. The family looked at winter coats for David and new dresses for the girls before heading downstairs for the bakery where they enjoyed a cup of coffee and Jordan Marsh's famous blueberry muffins overflowing with juicy berries with just a hint of lemon under that sugary topping.

Then on to the biggest challenge: Filene's bargain basement. Having now scouted the fashions and prices at the regular department store, the family searched for bargains and found new white shirts for the men, dresses for the girls, a new stylish felt hat for Valle. They picked out a few small things to mail to Norway; leather gloves, lace collars and cuffs to add to dresses, and handkerchiefs.

After this busy morning shopping, the family wound their way through the shoppers on Washington Street. The Lees stopped to admire the beauty of Park Street Church and made their way to the automatic luncheonette. Clutching their nickels and dimes the family slid the cafeteria trays down the counter as they picked out their sandwich and a dessert from the glass compartments before settling down rather cramped in the crowded restaurant.

"Look what I picked out," Harriet beamed with delight, "Look, it is a new kind of sandwich. It's a fish salad. It's tuna fish salad. The tuna comes in a can. I've had it once before, after a piano recital. Do you want to taste it?" The others declined but Valle was intrigued and tried a bite. "Tastes a little like chicken. Who would think it is so good?" Valle responded as she tasted the sandwich. "I'll be right back with drinks."

Just as Valle left to get some drinks, Harriet piped up, "Pa, I'm sorry but I bet this food at a luncheonette tastes better than that fish you have hanging in the cellar."

"Now look, David, girls, listen to me," his voice slowly got louder and louder, "Enough of this complaining. Your mother is homesick for Norway. She wants a nice Norwegian Christmas this year. She wants to eat lutefisk on Christmas Eve like she did as a girl. You will be kind to your mother. No more complaining about lutefisk. We will all enjoy the lutefisk. And we will all have a lovely Norwegian Christmas. Do you understand?'

"Yes, Pa..." they dutifully chorused.

The family finished their sandwiches and sampled each other's desserts, enjoying Trygve's Boston Creme Pie the most. The Lees returned to the stores and shopped for a few more gifts before traipsing back to the train station to head back home to Bolton, loaded down with their treasure and bargains.

The Fish

A few weeks later Trygve started soaking the dried fish. Trygve sawed the planks of dried cod into smaller sections to fit in the tubs he had prepared. David came down to see what his father was up to but quickly disappeared as the sawing seemed to release the pungent fish odor that already emanated throughout the house.

Trygve carried buckets of water down to the cellar to soak the fish. There was no drain or water source in the cellar. So, he had to either go up the stairs and through the tiny kitchen where Valle was cooking and baking to get to the sink or out the bulkhead stairs trying not to slosh water on his way to the backyard where the water froze into solid puddles. Back and forth, dumping fishy water out and adding fresh water.

Over the next few days, he continued draining the water off and adding fresh water as the dried cod plumped up, developing some flesh and filling up the buckets.

Then it was time to start the three days of soaking in the caustic lye solution. With his industrial strength black gloves on, Trygve mixed the ash and lye to the water. The fish had now enlarged so that both buckets were now overflowing with plumb white quivering cod fish. Trygve covered the buckets with a tarp and left them to soak.

Potatoes, Cookies, and Cod

Upstairs in the kitchen Valley was peeling potatoes. The large bag with 'MAINE POTATOES' printed on the sides was sitting on the counter. Harriet stood at the sink rinsing and cutting the potatoes before tossing them into a large pot.

"Ma, I thought we were making the lefse today."

"No, tomorrow. Lefse takes longer to make than you would think. The trick seems to be to get the dough the right consistency so the individual lefse don't fall apart when you flip them onto the pan. Boiling and mashing the potatoes a day ahead is supposed to help you get a firmer, drier mixture to roll out so you can cook it like a thin pancake. So after these boil I'll need your help mashing these up real good and then we'll cook the lefse tomorrow."

"I thought we were making more cookies tomorrow."

"Well, we can if we finish with the lefse. I have the fattigmann and sandbakkels all put up in tins. We can make whipped cream to fill the krumkaker on the 24th. I'll still need to make more pepperkake and butter wreath cookies. You can help with those.

That is five kinds of cookies. Now for a Norwegian celebration, we should have seven kinds of cookies.'

"Why seven?" David walked into the kitchen, looking at the pile of tins on the counter. "Can we try some now?"

"Sure," Valley rinsed and wiped her hands, "Here, these are the fattigmanns and I have plenty." She opened the tin and the cardamom scent effused through the kitchen. Dorothy had joined them and the family stood around savoring the fried cookies coated in powdered sugar.

"And you can each have one krumkaker. I need to save some so we have krumkakes left to fill with cream." So they each tried one of the delicate cookies cooked on a waffle like iron and rolled into a light golden cone.

"So why the seven cookies for Christmas?"

"I don't know. A tradition. We Norwegians have so many delicious cookies at Christmas, so for some reason every housewife is expected to make 7 kinds. Then you fill tins of seven kinds of cookies to exchange. Everyone has a different selection. I hope to bring mine to church to exchange. Of course, we have to pray for good weather if we are going to church. And talking about church, how is your rehearsing going for '*Jeg Er Sa Glad*' and maybe '*Silent Night*'? You could sing it in Norske."

"We'll have time to practice before church. How about the pepperkake? Where's the pepperkake? "David asked.

"I know that is everyone's favorite, isn't it?" Valle laughed, "No more left. We'll make some more. Now, let's finish mashing up these potatoes for the lefse making tomorrow. We'll get everything ready. It's soon Christmas Eve."

In the morning Valle began mixing the potatoes from yesterday and flour together for the lefse, adding a little cream and sugar, kneading the mixture, trying to make it into a ball but the mass of potato and flour would not hold together.

"Ma, what are you doing?" Harriet quizzically watched her mother.

"I have to make this into a dough that holds together a bit better. And then I will roll it out into a long log and cut the pieces even so they are all about the same size." She patted little flat ovals to roll out on the pastry board.

"But I do not have the big, flat lefse pan. I'm just using my fry pan. This may be more difficult to make than I realized. And this dough is too wet, I think," She looked worried as she added more flour. And more flour.

"This dough seems more gluey or runny than I think it should be," Valle also floured the kitchen table where she had stretched pastry cloth.

"This shouldn't be this difficult! After all, I make pancakes and pie crusts all the time." Valle had now begun rolling out the individual lefse which resembled crepe-like pancakes but were rolled out like pie dough.

"Maybe these are not the best potatoes for lefse," Valle mused as she struggled with mixing and kneading. The dough cracked and split. She added more flour to the rolling pin and pastry board.

"So, this is like rolling out a pie crust?" Harriet

asked.

"Yes, but lefse should be much thinner. Let me try to get this on the stove." Using a flat lefse stick, Valle tried to lift the dough and move it to the pan, but the lefse fell apart into three sections.

"Well, we will have lefse pieces, I guess." Valle rolled the pieces of the lefse pancake onto the hot fry pan and began rolling another lump of lefse dough onto the floured board to roll out. She patted it and shaped it and rolled it. This one stayed together. Back and forth, rolling out the circle of dough as thin as possible, lifting with a stick to lay out on the hot griddle, flipping it over to finish cooking, and lifting the lightly browned lefse in one piece to cool. Traditionally lefse is cooked on a large, flat unoiled griddle and the heat deliciously browns the thin lefse. Valle lifted the cooked lefse with a stick and then rolled the finished product onto a towel to cool. But few made it to the pan in one piece. And even fewer made it to the towel looking anything like a crepe. Even after cooking, getting the lefse off the fry pan and on to the towel to cool in one piece, there were few that held together.

Downstairs in the cellar, Trygve was still sloshing around with buckets of water. After first soaking the cod in water to plumb it up, he then soaked the gelatinous fish in the lye marinade for further softening. Now he was in the final stretch, soaking the fish yet again in clear water, this time to get all the lye out of the fish before final preparation of the lutefisk dinner.

The fish had plumbed up and multiplied like

the fish from a picnic basket on a beach in Galilee. Trygve had to remove the fish from the barrel, then draw out all the water, carrying buckets of water up the bulkhead stairs to dump it out outside onto the frozen ground. Each time he slowly walked up the stairs so as not to get the stairs wet and icy.

Trygve thought he was on the last trip. One last rinse and he hoped the lutefisk would be clear of lye and finally palatable and ready to cook. Trygve gave the bulkhead doors a heave open to the winter air, grabbed the last two buckets of water to discard, and made it up the stairs and out, only to have his feet slip from under him on the ice and land on his back, soaked in lye-fish-water, lying on the ice.

His whoop and holler brought the family running.

"Are you all right?" David was the first one there.

"Yes, oww...yes. Help me up...I'm not bleeding am I?"

David carefully positioned his feet on the icy ground to get leverage. "You are not bleeding Pa. Here, let me help you up." Trygve had rolled over and was on all fours as he tried to stand up. "Take my arm. Watch it. It's slippery." David instructed Trygve.

"I know that."

"Ma, stay away, I don't want you to fall too." David admonished Valle.

Trygve precariously balanced, hanging on to David's arm and said, "I'm OK. Nothing broken, I think I have a bump on my head. That's all."

"I am not bleeding," he added again.

Dorothy popped her head out of the stairwell, "Be careful Pa, it's slippery."

"I know that."

"Wow, is the ice extra slippery because it's frozen soapy water?" Dorothy asked.

Harriet and Valle stood in the cold shivering at a distance. All looked up to give Dorothy a blank look. Valle finally told her, "Dorothy, go back to where it is warm. We are all coming in."

"Well, I think soapy water would make ice even more slippery. Even I know that." And Dorothy disappeared into the house.

The remaining members of the Lee family carefully worked their way over to the back stairs and into the smoke-filled kitchen. One of the last of the lefse was crisping up black and giving up a circle of smoke. Valle grabbed a towel and the pan handle. Harriet leaned in and turned the stove off. Valle screamed and shook her hand. "Oh, my thumb and finger."

"You both need ice." David went out with a pan and filled it with snow.

Soon both parents were being iced. Trygve had a snowpack on his head and Valle had her thumb wrapped in an icy bandage.

"It's just my thumb. I'll be able to cook. Don't worry."

"Ma, we'll make more pepperkake. Don't worry."

"And I'll make sure the fish is well rinsed in clean water." David added.

"Well, it is almost complete." Trygve added. "We can just leave the fish in the fresh water, and I can continue taking care of it. I am fine. I just need a few minutes to ice this bump on my head. Uff da!"

The next morning Harriet mixed the pepperkake dough to chill. The small tree they had picked out for a Christmas tree was cut and placed on a table ready for decorations of tinsel and glass ornaments.

"I don't think packages from Norway will get here in time this year." Valle mused as she put a small star on the treetop. "I hope the weather holds out so we can get to church."

"The bread is in the oven." She added, "I do not think I am baking any more cookies this year." Valle looked at her bandaged thumb, "But we will have delicious lutefisk, so that will be good."

Christmas Eve Bolton

The morning sun never emerged. The gray slate sky covered a lightly frosted world that Christmas Eve. An icy drizzle polished the blanket of snow to a shining crust.

The smell of perking coffee filled the kitchen. Valle cut fruit filled Julekake bread and smothered the slices with butter. She also whipped up the eggs, milk, and butter to make waffles. There was soon a pile of brown waffles on a platter.

"Good morning, good morning," they greeted each other and helped themselves to bread and waffles covered in a light coat of white sugar.

"No cheese for the bread this year. I guess we will not have any packages from Norway in time for Christmas this year. Although I have some regular cheese from the store if any of you want that. Not quite the same as gjetost..." Her voice faded.

Trygve led them in a short grace. "Unless the sun shines and the temperature rises dramatically, we will not be going to church this afternoon. I am afraid it is too risky with ice and snow."

"Let's hope the sun shines soon." David said brightly. "We can practice the music anyways. We can hope and plan on going, can't we?"

His sisters looked rather glum and uninspired by his confidence.

"Well, if you are so inspired David," Trygve postulated, "Why don't you walk down to the train depot and get morning newspapers. Would you? I know it's slippery."

So everyone got dressed as if they would actually get out of the house that Christmas Eve. David bundled up in his winter's best and boots to slip and slide his way to the train depot and back.

Valle looked out and finally saw David and Major reappearing in the snow and rain.

"Woo, it's spitting sleet out there," Davis said as put down his packages and took off his wet coat and hat. "Here are the papers and look what I got Ma. Mrs. McCarthy was home and had something left to sell." David was grinning from ear to ear.

"Look, open the boxes Ma."

Valle opened the pastry boxes to uncover cookies.

"I went to Mrs. McCarthy's. And look, she had cookies left. No Christmas cookies left but look, snickerdoodles and hermits."

Valle looked up at her son with some confusion.

"The snickerdoodles are fresh. And the hermits are your favorite, Ma. With walnuts and dates." There was a moment of silence.

"Ma, now you have your seven kinds of cookies. Like you wanted."

Valle simply dropped the pastry box on the table and looked at her son.

She put her arms around David. "Of course. Oh, thank you. You are the best gift a mother could want." she said as her voice cracked. Tears streamed down her face. She wiped them away and tried to smile and offered, "Well if the snickerdoodles are fresh, maybe we should all try one."

Trygve put his hand on David's shoulder. "Thank you, son."

Later the Lee trio did indeed practice and sing the Christmas songs they would have sung at church. To an audience of two, they sang Christmas carols in English and Norsk. Valle prepared for the big dinner and hoped and prayed that this lutefisk meal would be edible. The table was set. The family listened to the radio as flurries filled the sky.

Then Harriet sat down at the piano and David and Dorothy leafed through her music sheets picking songs to sing. Harriet practiced *Rhapsody in Blue.* They sang *Yes Sir, That's My Baby* and they danced to *Charlston*, as Valle shook her head and Trygve gave a huge sigh and tried not to watch. Harriet was trying to see how fast she could play, and they could sing, *If You Knew Suzy Like I Know Suzy,* when the merriment was suddenly stopped by a deep pounding at the door.

Large clumping snowflakes filled the air outside. Dorothy was the first to the door. She looked out and turned to scream.

"It's Julenissen. Father Christmas is here!"

Father Christmas

Trygve opened the door and let the man in. The man, in a dark blue uniform, was covered with snow and loaded down with packages. Trygve brushed some of the snow off and the man stomped his feet. The visitor gave a hearty laugh and said, "Hey, Chris, sorry for startling your family like that with the banging. Boy, I could hear that singing and music coming from here halfway to Hudson! Believe it or not, it seems to be warming up. The roads aren't as icy as you would think."

"Joe, what brings you here on Christmas Eve? I didn't expect the post office would even be open."

"Well, no, we closed early today. But, well frankly Chris, I just had to get these packages out of the building. I couldn't get them out fast enough and deliver them to you. They are all from Norway. Sorry, but we couldn't stand the smell. We had to get them out of the building. I do not know what you have in here..."

"Cheese!" came the choral answer.

"And maybe fish," David added.

Valle turned to Harriet and spoke in Norwegian, "Get the man some cookie tins."

Then Valle turned to the postman, "A happy Christmas to you. Would you like something to eat?"

"Oh thank you Mrs. Lee but I have to get home to my own family. But thank you."

"Well please take some tins of cookies. Here, take both tins. We have plenty," Valle replied as Harriet arrived with the festive ribboned cookie tins.

Dorothy had appeared with a plate of goodies. "Here, sir," she said, "Try one of these. They are special lefse."

"Thank you, young lady." He picked up a triangle of lefse folded with butter and cinnamon. He bit in and chewed and chewed. "A little bit like pie dough? Yes?"

David grabbed a pepperkake cookie off the platter and offered it to their guest.

"Try these, they are, they are, spice cookies. Sort of like thin gingerbread."

"Oh, now that's delicious." The postman gave a wide smile as he munched on his cookie.

Then the guest added, "Thank you for the cookies. My children will love them. And a happy Christmas to you all. You are so fortunate to have your own Christmas concert right here in your home. I tell you, that was some great music. Take care of that cheese. Goodbye. Merry Christmas."

"Thank you for the delivery!" "Thank you and happy Christmas." "Merry Christmas".

The family turned their attention to the packages. Sure enough, there was plenty of their favorite cheeses, including the infamously smelly gamalost cheese. They unpacked all the cheese and laid them out for inspection. There were a few gifts wrapped in red tissue paper that went under the tree. And in the last package from the family in Halden, was the coveted gold wrapped box of liqueur filled Norwegian chocolates, like a gold gilded treasure box, Trygve held it up to admire.

With oohs and aahs from all, Trygve added, "Oh, we will save these for after dinner. And only one each!"

Valle finished cooking the lutefisk. The fish, butter, potatoes, meatballs, creamed peas, and mashed turnips were placed on the table. They bowed their heads and repeated grace together.

Trygve picked up the platter with the lutefisk, helped himself to a piece and then served his wife.

"Thank you," Valle smiled as she handed the platter on, "What a blessed Christmas Eve this is this year. I am so happy to have the packages from Norway in time."

Trygve smiled as he served himself spoonfuls of creamed peas. "This looks like a real Norwegian meal, Valle, what a feast." Trygve looked over the table at his smiling wife, his hungry children, and shook his head with a chuckle, "God bless us all. God bless America. Only in America would we get home delivery on Christmas Eve."

Barbara Belseth grew up in Hudson, Massachusetts surrounded by her warm extended Norwegian family. Beside 'the lake' where she spent summers with cousins and family, her favorite place was the library. Barbara studied English at UMass and then spent nearly 20 years aloft as a flight attendant for a major airline. She returned to the classroom to teach English to high school language learners. Retired today, after teaching students from over 50 different countries, Barbara lives in northern Virginia near her family and grandchildren, where she is involved with community bible study and writing and quilting.